"What The Hell Do You Think You're Doing?"

Slate bellowed as he strode toward the woman. He stopped suddenly, eyes narrowing. He didn't quite know what he'd been expecting. A female equivalent of Daniel Boone, perhaps.

She was attractive in a tomboyish way. Not the type of woman he was drawn to, usually, but not the type you'd expect to find setting mantraps in the mountains of British Columbia, either.

She was tall and slender and looked very capable and competent. And the easy way she held the rifle underlined the impression that she was more than able to take care of herself.

"Your move, sweetheart," he declared.

She blinked. Slate could have sworn he saw a glint of uncertainty in her eyes, gone before he could be sure. She wet her lips, and he suddenly realized that she didn't have the faintest idea what to do with him now that she'd caught him.

Dear Reader:

I hope you've been enjoying 1989, our "Year of the Man" at Silhouette Desire. Every one of the twelve authors who are contributing a *Man of the Month* has created a very special someone for your reading pleasure. Each man is unique, and each author's style, plot and characterization give you a different insight into her man's story.

From January to December, 1989 will be a twelve-month extravaganza, spotlighting one book each month with special cover treatment as a tribute to the Silhouette Desire hero—our *Man of the Month*!

You'll find these men who've been created by your favorite authors irresistible. Naomi Horton's Slater McCall is indeed *A Dangerous Kind of Man*, coming this April, and love, betrayal, greed and revenge are all part of Lucy Gordon's dramatic *Vengeance Is Mine*, featuring Luke Harmon as Mr. May.

Don't let these men get away!

Yours,

Isabel Swift
Senior Editor & Editorial Coordinator

NAOMI HORTON
A Dangerous Kind of Man

Silhouette Desire

Published by Silhouette Books New York

America's Publisher of Contemporary Romance

SILHOUETTE BOOKS
300 East 42nd St., New York, N.Y. 10017

ISBN: 0-373-05487-4

First Silhouette Books printing April 1989

NAOMI HORTON

Even as I wrote this book, my own construction hard hat sat on the end of my desk, inspiring me. I've always been fascinated by big construction projects and the men who work on them. As an engineering technologist, I spent my career working with engineers and contractors, but it was the two years I spent in northern Alberta on the Tar Sands megaproject that actually inspired this book—and my hero. Slater McCall is the essense of the construction gypsies who move from site to site, following the big projects from Brazil to Saudi Arabia to northern Canada.

Independent, restless, self-confident, they are in many ways the last romantic heroes. Like Slate, they are usually rugged individualists, who don't have time for social rituals and games. Yet most are true "gentle men" for whom chivalry is a code of honor. And even though I've left that life behind to write full-time, there will always be a part of me out there on an isolated construction site, listening to the wavering howl of wolves prowling the site perimeter as the northern lights whisper overhead.

For Ron
without whose help this book (and all the others)
would have been infinitely more difficult to write.
Thanks for your help, your humor,
your unflagging support and your incredible patience
(especially on those days
when your confidence in me exceeded my own).

One

He didn't even see the pit until he was in it.

One moment there was solid mountain under his boots, then, suddenly, nothing, as the inky maw opened under his feet and swallowed him alive. There was an instant of suspended time, of disbelieving terror, then only gut-wrenching vertigo as his worst nightmare became reality and he was falling into the bottomless, endless dark....

He hit solid ground. Off balance and blind in the utter darkness, he pitched forward and fell headlong into fresh, loose earth. It knocked the wind out of him and he lay there for a moment, motionless, tasting blood where his teeth had cut the inside of his lip. Gingerly, he looked up. A square of moon-grayed sky hung perhaps twelve feet above him, edges as cleanly cut as a new grave.

Then, with no more warning than a soft metallic click, the two halves of the camouflaged trapdoor that had fallen inward under his weight snapped back up as smoothly and tightly as the lid on a box.

He was caught.

* * *

Jamie wasn't quite asleep when Timber's large, wet nose nudged her hand. She was warmly cocooned in that delicious halfway state between dream and reality. Her father was there and they were talking quietly, their voices rising and falling above the crackle of wood on the hearth. The scent of his pipe wove its magic around her and she was laughing at something he said when the big dog whimpered.

She muttered in denial as the half dream started to unravel. Desperately she clung to it, somehow knowing that if she let it go, her father would go as well.

Timber nudged her again, and Jamie unwillingly opened her eyes as the last shreds vanished like smoke. With wakefulness came reality, the heart-wrenching knowledge that it had all been just a dream after all and that her father was dead as he had been for over a year now.

She sat up in the big armchair and rubbed her eyes, awake enough now to realize that the heathery scent of his pipe tobacco was real, emanating from the folds of the heavy flannel work shirt she'd pulled around her shoulders just before she'd dozed off. The whisper of the dying fire, too, was real. The pine knots she'd tossed into the fireplace against the evening's chill had burned down, leaving the cabin filled with the tart incense of pitch. But the rest had all been wishful thinking.

It took that sudden sting of grief to jolt her completely awake. Timber, the big husky-wolf cross that had been lying asleep on the woven rug by her feet, was gazing at her intently. He whimpered again and nudged her hand, and Jamie smiled and stroked his broad head. "What is it, old fellow? Did you hear something out there? A raccoon?"

The dog gave an impatient yelp and took her hand gently between his massive jaws, tugging. "What is it?" Jamie uncurled her feet from under her and fumbled for her slippers, frowning at the big dog's peculiar behavior. If someone or something was prowling around the cabin or he simply wanted out, he'd have had no trouble getting the message across.

He gave a sharp bark and stared up at her with such impatience that Jamie had to laugh. "Okay, okay—I'm coming. What do you want to show me?"

The dog bounded across the room and up the two broad steps into the dining area. He stood in front of the big desk, ears pricked forward, hackles raised, and broke into a deep-chested barking, glancing back at Jamie to see if she was coming.

"Timber, quiet! What on earth are you—?" She stopped dead, finally hearing an odd muffled sound and staring at the complicated array of lights and switches mounted above the desk. One of them was flashing an angry red, the pulsating glow reflecting eerily off the furniture and walls.

The alarm. The alarm she checked dutifully every morning for defects, the alarm she knew would never in a million years go off—*that* alarm was now flickering balefully at her.

"Oh, my God…." It couldn't be, she told herself calmly. It was an electrical short, that's all. A malfunction in the circuitry.

Or, another little voice advised her just as calmly, it could be the real thing.

"Oh, God!" She was up the stairs like a shot, scanning the board. The test circuits were glowing steadily, sanely green. If it was a malfunction, it was a damned selective one. "Timber, be quiet!" The dog whined, his wet nose twitching.

"Damn it, what's wrong with the sound?" Jamie gave the toggle switch a couple of flips, then noticed a roll of electric tape had gotten wedged against the bell. She extracted it and the shrill voice of the alarm cut through the air. Timber started barking furiously and Jamie yelled at him to be quiet even as she hit the switch again to cut the alarm. "Well, that's just great!" she muttered. If it hadn't been for

Timber, she might have slept right through until morning without being alerted.

Swiftly she keyed the necessary codes into the computer. The screen blinked passively for a moment, then spilled a silent display of answering codes across the screen.

It wasn't a malfunction. Something had triggered the circuit at the other end. Something tall enough to have broken the thin laser trip-beam set a good six feet above the forest floor, and heavy enough to have activated the weight-plate release on the trap itself. Both had to be triggered concurrently for the trap to open, a safety system she herself had invented after spending the first three weeks of operation racing around like a maniac resetting traps that had been sprung by every strolling bear and low-flying owl on the mountain.

That had been ten months ago. She hadn't caught a thing since.

Heart pounding, she snatched up her down vest and pulled it on, then struggled into her knee-high bush boots, stuffing the legs of her jeans into them impatiently. She cleared the computer screen, then reached for the radio microphone even while realizing there was no one she could call. Curtis was a good five hours away, enjoying his faculty dinner in Seattle, and Terry... well, her assistant had only a vague idea of what was going on here. He thought it had something to do with her study of the local bears, and she'd never bothered telling him the truth. For the time being, maybe it was better if she kept it that way. She was on her own.

But not alone. The big dog was sitting at attention by the door, his entire body quivering with barely suppressed excitement, and Jamie laughed softly. "Yeah, you're coming, too." As though understanding her, Timber bounced to his feet and started prancing, whining in his impatience to be underway.

Grinning, her own blood now racing with the same excitement, Jamie grabbed her rifle from its rack and slung it over her shoulder, stuffing a fistful of tranquilizer darts into the pocket of her vest as she headed for the door. Something made her glance at the other one, the big hunting rifle. There was a moment's indecision, then she turned her back on it and pulled the door open.

If she'd caught the bear she suspected she'd caught, there was no need for anything more than the tranquilizers. One well-placed dart would immobilize the animal long enough for her to secure the nylon webbing around it. Then she could use the winch on her Jeep to extricate the unlucky animal from its prison. And if it wasn't a bear...

Jamie swallowed nervously as she followed the bounding dog across the yard. There weren't many things big enough to trigger the trap wandering around these mountains, and of all of them, the bear was by far the most dangerous. Unless, of course, she'd finally caught what the trap had been designed to catch.

She pulled the Jeep door open, pausing long enough to check that her equipment was in the back. Timber hurtled by her and launched his ninety pounds into the Jeep as gracefully as a ballet dancer. He shoved his big face into Jamie's for an instant, then he was all taut muscle and pricked ears again, every one of his wolf senses aquiver as he assessed the night.

Trapped.

Slater McCall forced himself to take a deep, calming breath, swiftly taking inventory. A few bruises, but nothing broken. The padding of loose earth on the bottom of the trap had cushioned his fall, and although one shoulder felt slightly sprung and his left knee was going to be bothering him for a few days, he was essentially unhurt and in fighting trim.

Had there been anything to fight.

The darkness was like a shroud, thick as flannel. The air was pungent with the peaty smell of freshly turned dirt and he fought back a shudder, trying not to think of graveyards.

Cautiously he eased himself to his knees. He paused there, poised, but when nothing happened he got to his feet, staggering slightly, disoriented by the fall and the darkness. It was completely silent, the heavy, moist air deadening the sound of his harsh breathing. He held his arms out to either side, testing the dimensions of whatever he'd fallen into. His right hand met only air, but the tips of his left fingers brushed solid wall and he instinctively took a step nearer to it. His foot landed on something hard and cylindrical and he gave a grunt, scooped up the flashlight he'd dropped when the ground had opened up under his feet. He gave it a shake and it rewarded him with a burst of light that nearly blinded him.

Squinting, he swung the beam of light around him. And felt his heart drop.

Whoever had dug this pit trap had meant to keep whatever he'd caught. The walls weren't the dirt he'd expected, but heavy metal, slick with moisture. The seams had been expertly welded and smoothed so they wouldn't provide even the most rudimentary handhold. And they were angled, he realized with a sinking feeling as he swung the beam upward. The four walls of the trap canted inward near the top so even if the captured prey *did* manage to scale the slippery walls, it would never make those last few feet.

In spite of his predicament, Slate found himself admiring the engineering skill that went into the trap's design. "I don't know who you are, buddy, but when I get out of here, you've got a job if you want it." He swung the flashlight's beam around his prison again. "*If* I get out of here," he amended softly, his own engineer's mind estimating his chances.

Not good.

He played the beam of light across the trap lid, unable to discern even a crack where the two halves met. Solid steel plate, by the look of it, and heavy as sin itself. Yet they were so perfectly aligned that, closed, they looked like a single panel. Whoever had put this thing together was obviously no amateur. But what in the *hell* was he trying to catch?

There was nothing up in these mountains necessitating a trap of this size and complexity. Except for the bears, maybe. But if this thing was designed to trap bears, the trapper must be after the granddaddy of them all.

Jamie wheeled the Jeep in a half circle, then backed it expertly off the trail and between two pines so the twin beams of the headlights scythed across the trap. She left the motor idling and turned on the spotlight mounted on the upper brace of the heavy crash bars welded across the Jeep's grill. She jumped to the ground and gave the big winch mounted on the reinforced bumper a perfunctory check, then started toward the trap.

Timber was whining with excitement. The moment she'd stopped the Jeep, he'd rocketed out of it and was now tracking something intently, nose plastered to the ground, hackles stiff. He paused now and again when the scent trails confused him, then finally stopped at the edge of the trap and went into a frenzy of growling and barking, digging at the heavy steel door with his front paws.

"Timber!" Jamie gestured toward the Jeep. "Back off. Sit. And stay."

Timber whined, but a moment later he bounded toward the Jeep and sat down near it, eight years of training too deeply ingrained to be ignored.

Jamie realized that her heart was trip-hammering against her ribs. Drawing in a deep breath of cold night air, she started walking toward the trap, telling herself there was nothing to be afraid of. Whatever was down there was there to stay until *she* decided to let it out.

She knelt beside the trap and tugged the cover off what Curtis called her "spyhole." Taking a deep fortifying breath, she aimed her high-powered flashlight into the pit.

It was the click that alerted him. Slate looked up just as a peephole in the trap lid opened, and in the next instant he was blinded by the beam of a flashlight. He staggered aside, shielding his eyes with his arm, but before he even had time to figure out what was happening, the hole clicked decisively closed again. Then—nothing. No sound, no movement.

The sound of his rapid, harsh breathing filled his ears. He flicked his own light off and stood very still in the darkness, straining to hear something, his hand tightening instinctively around the solid grip of the flashlight. What in the *hell* was out there?

He swallowed, staring at the trapdoor. He'd distinctly heard an animal snuffling and growling up there, the click of heavy claws digging at the metal panel. He'd had a sudden nightmare of those doors falling open and depositing half a ton of irate grizzly on top of him; then whatever it was had gone away. There wasn't a sound up there now. Whoever had looked down at him obviously wasn't in a hurry to let him out. If he was going to let him out at all.

The possibility he'd been abandoned was like a fist in the pit of his stomach, driving his breath from him. Of all the horrifying options his mind had conjured up, he'd never considered simply being left here to die. The air was still reasonably fresh, so either those doors weren't as airtight as they looked, or whoever had built this trap had taken that into consideration, too. So he wasn't going to suffocate. Condensation on the walls would provide him with enough water to last for weeks, so it would be starvation or exposure that would get him—a solitary, lingering death, giving him plenty of time to think about it.

But he wasn't dead yet. Wiping the sweat off his face with his arm, he switched the flashlight back on and played it slowly over the walls and dirt floor of his prison, his mind already calculating, estimating. By God, he wasn't going to go down without a fight!

An echoing thud over his head startled him badly. He froze, instinctively turning the flashlight off. Dislodged dirt and pine needles rained down as footsteps—human, this time—crossed the steel doors. Next, from far away, came the unmistakable whine of a winch. The doors above him quivered, sending down another cascade of dirt, then one half of his prison roof folded back to reveal a star-speckled sky.

Slate didn't even realize he'd been holding his breath until it left him with a *huff*. A figure walked by the edge of the trap. Soon the other half of the door was drawn back. The figure stood by the edge of the pit, backlit so his features were invisible to Slate, simply staring silently down at his catch as though trying to decide what to do next.

Eyes narrowed, Slate gazed back up at his captor. Even knowing he was still at the stranger's mercy didn't take the edge off his relief at having something other than his own imagination to battle. "Hey! You!" The dark silhouette made no response, and Slate's tenuous patience suddenly evaporated. "What the hell are you waiting for?" he bellowed. "Get me out of here!"

"You clumsy idiot!" Jamie stared down at the trapped man in fury. "Of all the stupid—" The rest was lost under a tirade from the pit's depths, and Jamie wheeled away furiously. "Damn you drunken construction workers," she fumed, pulling the winch cable from the trapdoors. "You tear the town apart, roar up and down the roads like maniacs terrorizing every living thing within a fifty-mile radius and now you're stumbling around the mountains—" She gave the cable a ferocious pull, succeeding only in pinching her fingers. The pain brought tears to her eyes, making her madder than she already was.

"I'm not drunk!" The bellow practically rattled the steel doors. "I was just walking along when I fell into this...this thing!" The bellow, if possible, got even louder. "Now get me out of here!"

She was tempted, for one rash moment, to let him find his own way out. At first she'd been relieved to find that she'd caught a worker from the nearby dam site instead of the bear she'd half expected, but she was starting to wonder if she wouldn't have been better off with five or six hundred pounds of bad-tempered grizzly.

Because whoever was in her trap looked considerably more dangerous.

He was big, for one thing. A little too big, considering the mood he was in. And he was mad. There was no doubt about that. She'd heard the language often enough so it no longer shocked her, but she did recognize murderous fury when she heard it.

"Lady," the voice beckoned with deadly silkiness, "if you don't get me out of here within the next ten seconds, you'd better plan on leaving me here for good...."

The threat inherent in the words didn't need spelling out. Jamie paused, contemplating the wisdom of doing just that, when a sudden attack of human charity overrode caution. She muttered something under her breath that made Timber whimper and anchored the loosely woven net to the hook on the end of the winch cable.

"I'm throwing down some nylon netting," she called to her captive. "You can use it to climb out. Stand back...."

The silence was not promising. But it was too late now. Telling herself she was probably going to regret it, Jamie tossed the bundle of netting into the trap.

The net rippled down like silk, looking too fragile to support more than a sparrow. But a single touch convinced Slate that it would hold him and ten more like him, and he swarm up the makeshift ladder like a sailor up a ship's rigging.

It was, as he'd already guessed by the voice, a woman. She retreated to the shadows under the pines as he pulled himself up and got solid ground under him again. "What the *hell* do you think you're doing?" he bellowed as he strode toward her. "I could have broken my neck! Or was that the idea? Do you have a whole wall of trophy heads you've brought down with this—"

A low, deep-throated growl rumbled menacingly from the shadows near the woman's side. Slate stopped instantly, eyes narrowing. The dog—looked like a good hundred pounds of muscle and teeth—stepped from the shadows and placed himself between Slate and the woman. Its lips curled back and moonlight gleamed wetly on a set of fangs that could have crushed a man's arm as easily as a toothpick. The dog stared at Slate, the fur across his heavy shoulders rigid. Half-wolf, Slate estimated with instinctive admiration, maybe more. The pale eyes were alert and fiercely intelligent in the broad head, not threatening as much as giving warning.

"Easy, Timber." The huge animal acknowledged her assurance with a single wag of his bushy tail, but that burning gaze never left Slate's face and not a muscle relaxed.

Slate, caught in midstride, eased his weight back onto his right foot. The dog didn't move so much as a hair, and Slate let his breath out tightly. He didn't quite know what he'd been expecting. A female equivalent of Daniel Boone, perhaps. Davy Crockett in drag. Whatever he'd subconsciously thought to find, it sure as hell wasn't anywhere even close to the reality.

She was younger than he'd expected, for one thing. Mid-to-late twenties, probably, although it was hard to tell in the shadows under the trees. She was attractive, too, in a tomboyish kind of way. Not the type of woman he was drawn to usually, but not exactly the type you'd expect to find setting mantraps in the central mountains of British Columbia, either. She was tall and slender, enough of both that she could wear the bulky down vest and make it look like high fashion. Her slim-fitting jeans were stuffed into knee-high leather wilderness boots—the kind favored by city women for their stylishness and worn by this woman, he had no doubt at all, for their practicality in the bush. Under the vest she was wearing a flannel work shirt in traditional red-and-green lumberjack checks, open at the throat, the sleeves rolled back to her elbows.

She looked very capable and competent, and the easy way she held the rifle underlined the fact that she was more than able to take care of herself. It wasn't pointing at him. Quite. But he had the distinct feeling that if he made one wrong move, it would be. And there was something about the cool watchfulness in her eyes that made him just as certain that she knew how to use it.

"Your move, sweetheart."

She blinked. Slate could have sworn he saw uncertainty in her eyes, gone before he could be sure. She wet her lips, and he suddenly realized that she didn't have the faintest idea of what to do with him now she'd caught him.

"Well?" He snapped it out, using every bit of authoritative impatience he could muster. It was a voice honed over years of ramrodding some of the biggest construction projects in the world, and it usually got him the results he wanted.

"I—" Her eyes widened very slightly and she took a small backward step.

"I said, it's your move." He met her wide-eyed stare steadily. "You're the one holding the gun, sweetheart—I figure that puts you in charge."

"That's right." She said it a little too quickly, lifting the rifle fractionally. "I am."

"So?" He put his hands on his hips and stared at her, ignoring a rumble of warning from the big dog. "Do we get down to it right here, or are you going to take me home first?"

"Do we—what?" The last word was a squeak. Her eyes widened even more and she took another backward step.

"Come on, sweetheart," he coaxed with a laugh. "You've gone this far—don't tell me you're going to chicken out now."

She shook her head slowly, backing away from him. "I don't know what you're—"

Slate's grin broadened. "The way I see it, honey, no woman goes to this much trouble to trap herself a man unless she's real serious about it. I figure either we can strip down and have an encounter of the closest kind right here, right now—" he dropped his voice to a companionable purr, moving a casual step toward her "—or we can wait until we're somewhere a bit warmer. And softer. Slender little thing like you would get bruised something fierce on the ground like this." He dared another step toward her, trying to ignore the rising growl of warning coming from the shadows. "Unless you like being on top, of course. And hey—I have no problem with that. I like aggressive women—''

It had exactly the effect he'd counted on. Her eyes flew wide and she stared at him with her mouth half-open in shock, and even the shadows couldn't hide the deep blush that poured up from the neck of her work shirt. "I—it's—that's not what—damn you!" She caught herself, eyes practically giving off sparks as embarrassment gave way to anger.

"Okay, okay. I'll go on top," he said with an appeasing laugh, holding both hands up in surrender as he took another casual step toward her. "Hey, I'm easy."

It flustered her even more, exactly as it was supposed to, and in that split second he had her.

Two

Slate moved so swiftly she barely had time to suck in a startled breath before he'd whipped the rifle out of her hands and had swung her, hard, against the side of the Jeep.

"Timber, *down!*" His bellow coincided with a snarl of rage from the big dog and the animal stopped dead, whimpering in confusion. "Call him off, sweetheart."

"H-how did you do that?" She sounded as shaken as the dog.

Slate tightened his hold on her, hearing her breath catch. She was as supple as a cat, yet in spite of the tension in her body it was curved and soft where it should have been. His right arm had ridden up under the vest and he could distinctly feel the weight of her breasts through the soft flannel work shirt. He forcibly reminded himself that unless he kept his mind on what he was doing he was still in serious danger of losing a leg. Or worse. "I said, call him off."

She hesitated just long enough for him to get another deep breath of the green-grass scent of her hair. "Back, Timber," she said unsteadily. "It's all right. Back off. Sit."

The big dog whined, but after a moment or two did as he was told. Slate relaxed. "Good girl," he breathed. "Now I'm going to let you go, and I don't want any funny stuff, all right?"

Cautiously Slate eased his hold on her and stepped back. She slipped free of his grasp and faced him defiantly, still cornered against the Jeep, and for half an instant Slate thought she was going to launch herself at him.

Then she checked the impulse and relaxed back against the vehicle, rubbing her wrist where he'd been gripping it, and Slate gave a grunt of approval. "Wise move. I meant what I said about liking aggressive women—but I like 'em smart, too. You'll do."

"Thanks." Her voice was icy. She stepped away from the Jeep cautiously and when he made no move to stop her, she took a deep breath and relaxed noticeably. "Now what?" She sounded subdued, still massaging her wrist.

"First thing is to see what you've got in *here*." He cleared the chamber of the rifle and gave another grunt, this one of surprise as he removed the tranquilizer dart. He twirled it in his fingers, then slipped it into his jacket pocket and, without further ceremony, handed the rifle back to her.

She looked at it in surprise, then, almost tentatively, took it from him. They stood there facing one another for a long, taut moment, then she sighed deeply and turned to put the rifle in the Jeep. She switched off the headlights and cut the motor, and the darkness slipped around them. "How did you know Timber would respond like that when you shouted at him?"

"I didn't." Slate smiled at the expression on her face. "Calculated risk. He's obviously well trained, and I figured a loud and authoritative command would keep him off balance long enough for me to convince *you* to call him off."

One eyebrow lifted delicately. "If you're not drunk, you're crazy." There may have been the faintest hint of admiration in the words. "I could just as easily have ordered him to attack."

"But you didn't."

"No." She said it almost regretfully. "Another calculated risk?"

"That's right."

She looked at him for a long, thoughtful while. "What are you doing up here?"

"Walking."

"Walking?" She made it sound like the act of a madman.

"I like the mountains at night. They're quiet. Peaceful." He took a sidelong look at the trap. "Usually."

"I'd suggest you find yourself another nighttime activity," she said coolly. "These mountains are dangerous at night, even when you know them. Things can...happen. Especially to strangers."

He nodded toward the rifle. "Things like that?"

"Not usually," she advised him calmly, "but there are exceptions. And where you construction workers are concerned, it's becoming an option that's got its supporters. If I drove into town with you draped across my hood like an out-of-season buck, I'd probably get elected mayor."

The gibe went home. The lazy smile dropped from Slate's mouth and he gave her a hard, impatient stare. "Just what the hell do you townspeople have against the men out at the Skookum site, anyway? And what makes you think I'm one of them?"

"You've got dam written all over you." She let her gaze run deliberately over his jeans and worn leather jacket, pausing on the half-laced, scuffed work boots. "If you were local, I'd know you. If you were up here visiting someone, I'd know that, too. You're not in looking for work at the mills or mine site, because they're letting people go, not hiring. So that makes you an Outsider. And the only Outsiders we get up here have something to do with the Skookum Dam...and that makes them bad news."

"I suppose you're part of that conservation group that's trying to get us shut down, are you?" To his own surprise, he heard the ring of solid anger under his own words. He thought he was past that by now. Over the years he'd faced a lot similar groups, and although he often shared their concerns he could rarely share their simplistic solutions.

"My name's on the petition to stop construction, if that's what you mean," she said a trifle defensively.

"And maybe it was you who took a potshot at one of the riggers stringing cable on the high-tension towers across the valley last week? The bullet took a chip out of an insulator a foot from his head. Startled him so badly he lost his footing. If he hadn't been wearing his safety harness, he'd have come down off that tower onto solid rock, leaving a widow and three kids."

"I did no such thing!"

She said it with such indignant outrage that Slate believed her. He smiled grimly. "Well, someone from your friendly little community did. Rigging high-tension cable is dangerous work at the best of times; they don't need someone shooting at them to liven things up." He thought she was going to say something for a moment, then she subsided. "Anyway, we never did resolve what you're going to do with me now you've caught me. Sure you don't want to take me back to your mountain cabin to—?"

That square little chin lifted a defiant notch. "Don't push it," she said precisely. "I could shoot you yet, and call it self-defence."

Slate found himself laughing, as much at the woman's defiance in the face of defeat as at the blush that lightly glazed her cheeks. How long had it been since he'd seen a woman blush? He'd forgotten how appealing it could be, how that tantalizing hint of innocence could quicken a man's interest.

Her eyes were wide and dark—and green. How he knew they were green, he had no idea. But he knew. With the same certainty that he knew the torrent of hair tumbling around her face and shoulders was the high-voltage red of copper wire. "Don't be too quick to toss me back, angel. With the mine and mill closings, most of the eligible men have hightailed it out of the valley looking for work. I hear the pickings are pretty slim." His grin broadened. "Never can tell, sweetheart. I may be what you've been looking for all your life."

"I'm sure the thought appeals to your caveman ego, but you're not even close to what I'm looking for."

Again, Slate found himself grinning, starting to enjoy himself. "Aren't you even a little curious about what you might be missing?"

"Trust me," she shot back. "I'd rather be coated with honey and staked out naked in grizzly country." She spared him a cool glance as she stepped by him and strode toward the trap.

The big dog fell into step beside her, giving Slate a glance nearly as chilly as the one his owner had tossed him, and Slate watched the two of them walk toward the trap, unable to wipe the grin off his face. For some reason the image of this redheaded, rifle-toting spitfire naked, marinated in honey or otherwise, struck him as unexpectedly appealing. Other thoughts followed, thoughts remarkable not for their blatant eroticism but for the fact that he was thinking them at all.

He'd learned his lesson a long time ago and had made a hard-and-fast rule—one that lapses of judgment over the years had only reinforced—of *never* getting involved with the local women. It wasn't always an easy rule to remember when a man was working on a construction site in the middle of nowhere for months on end, but in the long run it sure as hell paid off.

The delectable pairing of well-worn denim and rounded female buttocks managed to distract him for a moment as his captor strode purposefully away from him, but Slate managed to tear his gaze away, reminding himself that a nicely shaped bottom didn't alter the fact that she'd nearly killed him. He followed her to the pit and pulled up the netting, thinking thoughts guaranteed to cool his fantasies. Poor Alison: she could hardly have guessed when she'd married him, that one day she'd have the same effect on him as an icy shower.

The woman looked across the open trap at him, obviously annoyed that he'd followed her. Slate wadded the netting up and tossed it at her. "Pit traps. Nets. Trank darts. Whatever the hell you were expecting to find out here, sweetheart, it was going to give you more of a fight than I would have." He grinned at her. "Still time to change your mind."

"Drop dead," she said almost absently, shaking out the net and starting to fold it meticulously. "I was hoping to find ... I was expecting to find a bear."

The way she faltered made Slate look at her. "You make a habit of messing with grizzlies in the middle of the night?"

"Black bear, not grizzly," she replied, still sounding distracted. "We don't get grizzlies up here. Not often, anyway."

"We've had an invasion of bears out at the camp," he said without thinking. "They're causing a lot of trouble."

The woman looked up at him, dark eyes flashing. "Of course they're coming around the camp! You've got nearly five hundred men working and living out there. You've got a trailer camp adjacent to the dam site the size of a small town, complete with recreation facilities and some of the best food in the world. Food means garbage, and garbage means bears. If you'd airlift it out as you were told to instead of just tossing it on the construction refuse dump, you wouldn't have this problem."

"Lady, the cost of airlifting garbage is not in my budget!"

"Well, I hope your budget is flexible enough to cover the cost of emergency airlifts to a hospital. Your site doctor can handle broken bones and crushed toes, but if one of your men tangles with a bear sow protecting her cubs, the only place with the facilities to take him is Kelowna."

"I'm aware of that," Slate told her testily. "We're fencing the dump off, as a matter of fact."

She gave a ladylike snort and tossed the net down. "These bears have been out of hibernation only a few weeks, and they're half-starved. The only fence that'll keep a nursing and hungry sow out of that dump will cost you more to put up than the entire dam itself.''

It wasn't something he needed to hear. He'd already had this argument with Sam Two Elks and he wasn't in any mood to have it again halfway up the side of a mountain with a well-armed and obviously unsympathetic bear trapper. Or whatever she was. He started brushing dirt and pine needles off his jeans and shirt front, and a moment later glanced up to find the woman watching him with a worried frown. Her gaze drifted to his right temple and he put his hand up, surprised to encounter a sizable lump. He brought his fingers away smeared with dirt and blood and he stared at them in surprise.

''You must have hit your head when you fell,'' she said quietly, her eyes troubled. ''I...well, I could clean it, if you like. Put something on it to stop the bleeding.''

''You've done enough already, thanks. In fact I think I'm going to find my way down this damned mountain before you change your mind and I wind up skinned and dressed, with my head mounted over your mantelpiece.''

She flushed, the faint concern vanishing under a spark of anger. ''If you hadn't been trespassing, you wouldn't have fallen into this thing in the first place. You've got no business being up here. Skookum Mountain is private property.''

''Isn't there a law against trapping out of season?'' he reminded her calmly. ''I bet the Conservation boys would be interested in this little setup of yours.'' She didn't answer him, but a tightening around her mouth told him he was hitting pretty close to home. He wandered across to the tall pine just adjacent to the trap, nodding toward the small black box strapped securely to the trunk about six feet above the ground. A beam of light about the diameter of a pencil lead shone across the trail to an identical box on the other side of the trap. He held his hand up to break the beam. The trip mechanism in the trapdoor clicked, and Slate's smile widened.

"Neat little setup. Laser trip and weight-plate to open the doors, explosion pins to slam them closed after your prey is deposited safely inside. Expensive, though." He strolled back to the pit and knelt beside it, running his fingers along the smooth metal of the door. "Damned expensive. Every time it's triggered, those explosion pins have to be replaced. Then the doors have to be reset, the whole site tidied up." She didn't deny any of it, but merely stared down at him as though seriously wishing she'd never bothered to pull him out at all. "So, what's the story? Some secret government study? Military?"

She gave a snort of laughter that was half dismissal and half relief. "You should get a job writing best-sellers."

Not government, he decided. Something private. And something secret. She looked up just then and caught him watching her. The clouds scudding across the moon shadowed her face and eyes, but Slate caught the gleam of cool speculation in them, felt the hair along his neck stir just slightly. The animal by her side shifted uneasily and lifted its heavy muzzle to scent the wind. Then, abruptly, she turned and walked toward the Jeep.

"There aren't any more of these between here and home, are there?" he called after her.

"Not if you stick to the trail."

"Does that mean there are others out here?"

"Stick to the trail." She stepped into the Jeep. "And stay off these mountains, if you know what's good for you. There are things out here you don't want to mess with."

Something about the way she said it made a little unexpected shiver run between Slate's shoulder blades. "Bears?"

There was a long pause. Too long. "Bears, too," she finally replied. "Just stay off my mountain and you'll be all right."

My mountain. Slate stared thoughtfully into the darkness where the last flicker of taillight had vanished, leaving him alone and in utter silence. *Things you don't want to mess with.*

A piercing cry cut through the night air and he started badly. Something drifted over his head and he caught the whisper of wind through feather, sensed more than saw the heavy downbeat of wing. Then it was gone and he started breathing again. He gave a snort of tight laughter and shook his head at his own jumpiness, heading back down the trail toward the dam site. There was nothing up here. Nothing but an owl or two, a few sleeping bears and a madwoman with a tranquilizer gun and a penchant for trapping strangers.

Slate stood at the door of the big trailer that acted as his office, hands on hips, and surveyed the huge construction site sprawling in all directions. *His* site, he found himself thinking. *His* dam. He felt much the same proprietary pride that a conquering warlord must feel on gazing over hard-earned and well-won kingdoms.

He smiled at the image. He hadn't fought for this kingdom. In fact, he'd fought a hard but losing battle *not* to take it. He'd been down in Brazil ramrodding another dam across another wild mountain river with a name he never did learn how to pronounce when the head office boys at Monolith Contractors had called him home.

The project engineer at the Skookum back then had been Charlie Cornelius, and during the two years he'd been here things had gone—in their words—to hell. Realizing that keeping Cornelius on the job was jeopardizing the entire project, they'd given Slate little choice in the matter. "That's what comes," he'd been told unsympathetically, "with being one of the best project engineers in the business." When he'd named another half dozen just as good or even better, they'd ignored him and had handed him a plane ticket to Vancouver. "The Skookum's in trouble," was all they'd said. "And it's your job to fix it. Just bring it in on time, McCall. That's all you have to do."

Sure.

The sad part of the whole thing was that he loved this business. Loved every miserable gut-wrenching, back-breaking part of it.

He shoved his hard hat back and took a deep breath of warm spring air, tasting mud and diesel fumes and smiling at the familiar bite. Like any big construction site, this one resembled a cross between a war camp and a frontier boomtown. To the inexperienced eye it was a hodgepodge of supply shacks and construction trailers, massive piles of pipe, bales of wire and huge, indescribable pieces of equipment that would look more at home in a science-fiction movie. Mud-spattered trucks buzzed everywhere, playing tag with massive pieces of earth-moving equipment. And, dominating everything, the dam.

As always, it made his breath catch. It soared above him, curved and pale and beautiful against the sun, pressing outward against the shoulders of confining mountain to either side and upward against the sky. It was still harnessed with a webbing of catwalks and scaffolding and cranes, its flanks cluttered with equipment and men, yet the sheer immensity of it could be in no way diminished. The lines of it were pure and clean against the spring sky, every angle perfect, every long, clean curve breathtaking in its simplicity and power. And it was his.

"Lord of all he surveys."

Slate started slightly. He looked down to find Bill Moss grinning up at him, and had to laugh. "Is it that obvious?"

"You look at that dam like most men look at a woman."

Slate grinned back and wandered back to his desk. It was half-hidden by stacks of thick, bound reports and scheduling sheets, letters and field memos, half-rolled electrical blueprints and overstuffed file folders secured with elastic bands. It looked like a hopeless mess, but Slate knew its layers and hummocks the way a trained archaeologist knows his dig.

Bill stepped up into the trailer and tossed his hard hat and clipboard down, then poured himself a mugful of coffee and sat down. "So, how does it feel to be back in charge of a *real* dam?"

Slate's growled reply was both heartfelt and profane, and Bill laughed. He set his feet on the corner of Slate's cluttered desk, crossed his ankles and tipped the chair back until the springs squealed in protest. "Well, I'm glad to see you haven't lost your touch since we last worked together. You've been on this project—how long now? Three weeks? And already a couple of dozen guys have walked off the job, two supervisors have quit, four unions are threatening strike action and word's out there's a price on that pretty head of yours would make even an old buddy like me think twice."

Slate laughed and set his muddy, boot-shod feet on the desk across from Bill's. "Cornelius ran this project like a gypsy camp for the past two years. Can't expect head office to bring a new man in without ruffling a few feathers."

Bill gave a gargantuan snort. "When we got word head office was sending you in to take over, there was a lineup a mile long of guys wanting out. They call you The Terminator, son."

Slate grinned lazily, well aware of what he was called behind his back. "The Terminator" was one of the least creative but by far the most printable of the lot. "The only people who walk off a job when they see me coming are slackers and troublemakers, and we don't need either. And the unions are just raising a dust storm to save face. Cornelius let their guys get away with murder for two years and they know it. Couple of days from now they'll settle back down to work and never mention it again."

Bill gave a grunt. "Too bad it took head office two years to figure out that Cornelius couldn't handle a project this big. It's going to be one hell of a year and a half, trying to get this dam finished on schedule. You're going to have to ride these boys like a slave driver."

"If necessary." Slate said it quietly, but he knew Bill heard the steel in his voice. "The penalty clauses alone will bankrupt us in three months if we don't meet those schedules." He pulled his hard hat off and tossed it onto his desk, scrubbing his fingers through his sweat-matted hair. "Monolith is one of the biggest dam contractors in the world, but all it takes to ruin a reputation is one or two botched projects. If word gets out that Monolith doesn't have what it takes anymore, you and I won't be able to get jobs digging drainage ditches."

Bill nodded. "Yeah, it's a mess, all right. I'm glad you're on board, old buddy."

"Thanks," Slate replied dryly. He reached for the mug by his elbow and took a swallow of the strong coffee. That's the first thing he'd done on taking the Skookum project over: there wasn't a trailer or supply shed on-site without a big percolator and as much freshly brewed coffee as the men could drink. It was one of those seemingly insignificant things he'd learned years ago. He had men out there pouring concrete twelve hours straight, others working high steel or operating the huge cranes that hung out over the half-finished dam like birds of prey or doing any one of a thousand other dirty, brutal jobs. A simple thing like hot coffee could make the difference between a man just doing his job—and doing his best. And all Slater McCall ever expected was a man's best.

He glanced up to find Bill staring at him speculatively. "Some of the men have got a wager riding on whether or not you're going to be able to pull it together in time to meet deadline. Some figure head office left it too late, that even Killer McCall ain't gonna be able to bring her in on time."

"She'll come in on time," Slate assured him in a lazy drawl.

"Who was that three-piece suiter underfoot the last couple of days? Someone said he's from the mayor's office from that smudge on the map over yonder they call a town. Place is so small I didn't think they'd even *have* a mayor."

"The good folk of Pine Lake would have your head on a spike in the town square if they heard you say that," Slate said with a chuckle. "They've got two churches, a post office, a pool hall, three stores and a gas pump and they're proud of all of it."

"Not to mention three bars and a handful of ladies of questionable repute. Or so," Bill added with a grin, "I've been told. And speaking of which—"

"—speaking of which," Slate picked up smoothly, "you read that memo right. Pine Lake is off limits from today on. No exceptions without my approval."

Bill gave a long, low whistle. "You're going to step on some toes with that one, son. Lot of our guys go to town after shift to blow off a little steam, have a couple of beers, high step a bit with the local lovelies. You make that ruling stick and you're going to have the rumblings of serious rebellion."

"Let them rumble. I've got a stack of complaints from the locals two feet high about drunk construction workers tearing the town apart night after night, fighting, making nuisances of themselves with the women. The police know half our camp by name. And those ladies of questionable repute moved in from Vancouver to set up business specifically for our benefit, and most of the community's pretty mad about that, too."

Bill gave a grunt. "Where you have construction camps, you have ladies of the evening. Hell, camp followers date right back to antiquity—even Caesar had 'em." He grinned slyly. "Remember that setup Rosie and her pals had in New Mexico? Until you turned prude and shut it down, anyway."

Slate had to laugh. Three enterprising prostitutes from a nearby city had bought a camper-trailer and had set up business right outside the construction-site gates. "I didn't turn prude," he drawled. "But the waiting line got so long it was interfering with traffic going on and off the site. I had to do something."

Bill laughed. "Security tells me you're cracking down on them, too."

"What security?" Slate gave his head a slow shake. "Site security's been a joke for the past two years—there isn't even a guard on the front gate half the time. People wander on and off the site like tourists at a summer fair. We've got one old local who drives his truck in every couple of days and 'borrows' whatever he needs—lumber, tools, even gas and parts for his truck.''

"That the old guy I see now and again fishing off the end of the upper coffer dam?''

"That's him.''

"Damn!'' Bill said with respect. "You seen the trout that old boy pulls in? I've been meaning to ask him what kind of flies he uses, but—'' He stopped, his face falling. "Don't tell me you're keeping him out, too?''

"Him too. This is a construction site, not a church picnic.''

"Hey,'' Bill protested with a laugh, "you're talking to a believer, remember? I'm one of the people who spent my winter getting you brought in off that Brazilian job to take over here.''

Slate had to smile. "I don't know whether to thank you—or shoot you.''

"You'll thank me eventually.'' The chair protested loudly as Bill shifted. "This dam's going to make you a hero, son. You're going to go down in history as the man who tamed the Skookum.''

"General George Armstrong Custer went down in history, too.''

Bill gave a gust of laughter and pulled his feet off the desk. They hit the floor with a thud and the entire trailer shuddered, dust drifting like fairy glitter in the sunlight trickling through the window. The chair squealed as he got to his feet. "Well, as much as I'd like to stay here and tell you how to run this operation, I gotta go to work. And you got real trouble heading this way any minute now. Figure I'd like to be clear when she hits.''

"When what hits?'' Slate looked up. "What kind of trouble?''

"The worst kind,'' Bill retorted with a sly grin. "Woman trouble. On the hoof, and mad as hell.''

Slate winced. There was only a handful of women working on-site, most of them laborers, heavy equipment operators and welders. Outnumbered a hundred to one by the men they worked with, they were the kind of hardworking, serenely competent women who didn't get ruffled easily. If he had one of them mad at him, it was serious. "Now what?" he sighed.

"I didn't hang around long enough to find out," Bill told him with a chuckle. "I just know there was a woman out at the front security gate mad enough to char stumps asking where she could find one Slater J. McCall. Thought I told you never to promise 'em anything you might not want to deliver, old son."

"I haven't been promising anybody anything," Slate assured him. He shook his head, completely mystified. "Beats me."

Bill glanced at his watch. "Well, I figure you'll find out in about three or four minutes. I'm gone." He settled his hard hat over his thatch of unruly brown hair and headed for the door. "Don't let 'em grind you down, son," he said over his shoulder. "The Skookum Curse has gotta lift sooner or later."

"What the *hell*," Slate asked himself aloud, "is the Skookum Curse?"

"Old Indian curse put on mountain and valley," a guttural voice answered him. "Protect river from white man's dam."

"What?"

Sam Two Elks, grinning broadly, stepped up into the trailer and tossed a handful of files onto Slate's desk. Dropping the phony Saturday-matinee Indian accent, he said, "This whole project's been cursed from the start—two men killed, equipment breaking down, the whole thing nearly six months behind schedule."

"All of which can be explained by bad site management, not curses," Slate reminded him dryly.

Sam gave a grunt of grudging agreement. He settled his stocky body on one corner of the desk and looked at Slate, his black eyes glinting with faint disapproval. "Your new security regs have irritated the Conservation people."

"What? Damn it, Sam, I've bent over backward to cooperate with them! I've given them an office on-site and provided space where they can run tests for air and water contamination. I've assigned two full-time staff to help them tag salmon during the spawning run and work up designs for the fish ladders and hatchery that *I* convinced the British Columbia and Washington State hydroelectric companies to finance jointly. I—"

"You had two biologists kicked off the site yesterday."

Slate stopped in midprotest. "Escorted off the site," he corrected a bit touchily.

"You white men always did have a talent for playing with words, McCall. Remember that the only difference between a heroic victory and a bloody massacre is which side you're on."

Slate ignored the dig. "The camp dump site is off-limits to everyone—it's too dangerous with all those bears prowling around. And I'm sure as hell not having two biologists wandering around this construction site as though they own the place."

"They say the dump is a perfect place to study the bears."

"The dump is within the confines of the construction security perimeter, Sam. That makes it off-limits to outsiders."

"Big mistake, Paleface."

"Off-limits," Slate repeated firmly.

"Have it your own way, McCall," Sam said with a chuckle. He tapped his knuckle against one of the folders he'd brought in. "There's the proposal for the recreation center and hockey rink the Native Action Committee worked up. Think we'll get it?"

Slate smiled. "This dam is a joint Canadian-U.S. venture as part of the Columbia River Treaty, Sam. Both governments have already had all the flack they need from every civil rights and environmentalist group in existence. They'll jump at a chance to be seen doing something positive for the valley's indigenous people. It's good PR."

"Watch who you're calling indigenous, Paleface," Sam said, grinning, as he headed for the door. "Gotta go, man. And good luck, McCall," he shot back over his shoulder on his way out. "You're going to need it."

Slate was still puzzling over Sam's last remark when someone he only half recognized as one of the site security staff hit the door to his trailer at a dead run. He was flushed and perspiring heavily, and he looked badly rattled. "I tried to keep her out, Mr. McCall. I told her she couldn't just come in here like this. I told her she had to have a pass. I told her she—"

"Calm down." Slate held up a restraining hand. "Now, who—?"

"That biologist," the man said breathlessly, slipping a fearful look over his shoulder as though the very devil himself was out there. "That one we kicked off the site yesterday."

"Escorted off the site," Slate corrected wearily.

"*Kicked* off the site," came an irate voice from behind the security guard. "And will you tell this idiot to get out of my way!" The voice, crystal bright with anger and coming right on his heels, catapulted the guard across Slate's office.

There was a flurry of activity just outside the trailer, a piercing wolf whistle, raucous shouts of male approval, then a tall, slender figure burst through the door, the sunlight glowing off hair the color of polished copper. "Just who the *hell* do you think you are, telling me that I can't—" She stopped dead, green eyes widening. "Oh, my God!"

Three

———

Oh, Lord,'' Slate echoed, wondering if both pleas for divine intervention would reach the right ears at the same time and, if so, which would be heeded first. He rubbed his eyes, suddenly realizing that at some deep gut level he wasn't really surprised. Lifting his head, he stared at her, perplexed curiosity and outright annoyance shooting through him as their eyes met. Damn it, he had a bad enough day ahead of him without *this*. "I should have known it was you."

"You! You—!" Her fury had taken her well beyond words and she simply sputtered for a moment or two, then drew in a deep breath in preparation for another attack.

"Lady," Slate grated dangerously, "if I were you, I'd be plenty careful about what you say. You're on *my* turf now."

It seemed to defuse her. Calming herself with a visible effort, she strode across to stand squarely in front of him. "My assistant and I were *escorted* off your site yesterday afternoon and told not to come back and I damned well want to know why."

It took him every ounce of willpower he had not to laugh. Not that it was even remotely funny, God knows. All he needed today was a wild-eyed, gun-toting biologist tearing the place up. But there was something about her....

Maybe it was her eyes, just as green in daylight as he knew they'd be. They were wide and thickly lashed and so incredibly expressive that the anger in them was almost palpable. He had no doubt at all that given the right circumstances, they'd be as warm and inviting as smoked jade. She was wearing a pale blue denim work shirt today, sleeves rolled up, top three buttons undone to expose the leather thong and heavy, crescent-shaped pendant she was wearing around her throat.

It took him a moment to realize it was a polished bear's claw, secured to the thong with a narrow band of handworked silver. A matching thong secured the end of the single braid that hung over her left shoulder to rest on the upper swell of her breast. The humidity had made her hair curl and a nimbus of copper-red tendrils had escaped from the braid, framing a face that was an intriguing blend of fragile beauty and fierce strength. Her jeans were businesslike and unadorned by designer names, and they fit her, Slate couldn't help noticing, the way God had surely intended jeans to fit.

Big mistake. As mad as she was, she hadn't missed the way his gaze had perused her, lingering appreciatively here and there, and when he finally drew his gaze back up to hers she was practically giving off sparks.

Apologizing made even less sense than pretending it hadn't happened, so he simply held her gaze steadily and wondered idly if she was going to give in to the obvious urge to take a swing at him or not.

How she managed not to plant her open palm across Slater McCall's handsome face, Jamie honestly didn't know. She'd never slapped a man in her life before, had never imagined herself even capable of such an act. But there was something about the way he was looking at her, something about the lazy arrogance in his eyes that said he knew damned well what she was thinking and literally *dared* her to do it, that sent her distaste for violence out the window.

But it wasn't just a distaste for violence that kept her hands at her sides. She'd spent too many years studying large, dangerous carnivores not to have a healthy respect for the male animal in any guise, especially on his own territory. And this one was just a little too big and a little too unpredictable to take a chance on.

Here, in daylight and in the confines of a construction trailer, the man was even taller than he'd looked three nights ago. His height made him look deceptively slim, but the shoulders and chest under the red-and-white checked shirt were rock solid and his deeply tanned forearms, bared by his rolled-up sleeves, were corded with muscle. But it was his eyes that unnerved Jamie the most. Pale textured gold, they were shrewd, almost calculating, and they held hers with a penetrating intensity that made her feel as though every secret she'd ever had was his for the taking. Wolf eyes.

Through a sheer battle of wills, she managed to hold that steady stare. "I'm an ethologist with the—"

"A *what*? I thought I'd heard of every 'ologist' there is, but that's a new one."

"An animal behavioralist," she explained with feigned patience. "I'm working with the B.C. Department of Fish and Wildlife, doing a study of stress in black bears under a grant from the University of Washington."

There was no response. Not even a flicker in the amber eyes holding hers. He was half sitting on one corner of a battered old desk, long legs spread aggressively and thrust out to either side so he was almost straddling her, and Jamie was starting to feel trapped. The silence pulled so tight it almost sang. "I've been working with a group of bears in the—"

"I didn't quite catch your name."

It was designed to knock her off balance, and it very nearly succeeded. But she managed, somehow, to hang on to her temper. "Kilpatrick. Jameison Kilpatrick."

He smiled, very faintly. "Okay, Irish, let me spell it out for you. As of three days ago, no unauthorized personnel are allowed on-site without security passes, hard hats, safety boots and one hell of a good reason for being here."

"I *have* a good reason! I've been coming in to that dump every day for the past two months, and—"

"Not any more."

"Damn it all, you can't just—"

"Sweetheart, I can do anything I please." There was a matter-of-fact bluntness to it that made Jamie blink. "This is *my* site, got that? This is a construction site, not a private wildlife preserve set up for your convenience."

"But I had an agreement with Charlie Cornelius that—"

"Charlie Cornelius isn't in charge here anymore." He stood up and Jamie took an involuntary step back before she could catch herself. "I am."

"Oh, for heaven's sake!" Jamie wheeled away from him. "Your dump isn't even *on* the site, technically—the security fence doesn't extend that far around. I can do like the bears do and just walk in from the logging road leading to the river. I don't have to come anywhere near your precious dam!"

"You can't fence in a river and half a mountain," Slate drawled as he sauntered around his desk and sat down, "but it doesn't take a rocket scientist to know that whole area is site property, fenced or not." The chair squealed as he tipped it back and braced one foot on the edge of the desk, gazing at her across his upraised knee. "I'm sure someone with a degree in ethnology can figure it out."

"Eth-*ol*-ogy."

"Whatever."

Resisting an urge to scream, Jamie walked across to his desk. "Mr. McCall, I've been working with the bears in this valley for nearly four years. I've tagged and catalogued over fifty individuals and I've got radio-tracking collars on twelve of them. The past four years of work have just been determining baseline behavior patterns. From that, I can determine when a given bear's behavior deviates from its specific normal response. As I said, my study is specifically aimed at how bears react to stress—particularly when that stress is caused by their sudden proximity to man. If—''

"Honey, I don't care if you're handing out Valium. Just as long as you do it outside the perimeter of my site."

"But, damn it, that's the whole point!" Jamie gestured impatiently. "Your dump site has created an absolutely perfect study environment. You've drawn bears in from all over these mountains. They're all coming under unbelievable stress—the local bears through having their territory invaded, the strange bears through doing the invading, all of them stressed by the activity associated with this dam. I couldn't have *designed* a better setup if I'd tried!"

He just gazed back at her implacably, and Jamie felt her temper start to get the better of her. "If you cut me off from the dump—if I can't observe them while they're in close proximity both to each other and to the dam, all of them in competition for the available food—then I may as well pack up and go home!"

"And if one of those cute little critters decides to try biologist on the half shell for lunch?"

"Oh, for—!" Jamie took a deep, calming breath. "Mr. McCall, I've been around bears all my life. I know the bears in these mountains better than most people know their own family. I am *not* going to get eaten. And besides, why would you care if—"

"Honey," Slate cut in with a silken smile, "it's not your cute little butt I'm worried about—it's mine. If one of those bears scatters pieces of you up and down this mountainside, or even if it just mauls you enough to put you in the hospital for a couple of months, I'll have enough lawsuits coming down on me to pave the road from here to Pine Lake.

"Even if we don't get sued, it'll take me six months just trying to explain to my bosses and the two hydroelectric companies who contracted this dam, not to mention both the U.S. and Canadian governments, why I allowed a wildlife biologist unrestricted access to the site in the first place.

And we haven't even *discussed* the fact that I'll be up to my neck in safety inspectors and union reps and reporters and television crews." He sat up, his boot hitting the floor with a thud that made the windows rattle. "And, lady, I just don't need the hassle. On a project this big, trouble has a way of creating itself—I sure as hell don't have to go out looking for it."

"But I can sign something—a waiver relieving you and your company of any responsibility if anything happens to me."

"To coin a phrase, honey, a waiver isn't worth the paper it's written on. It might keep your family from suing me personally for negligence, but it isn't going to keep the mud from hitting the fan." He grinned fleetingly. "So to speak."

Jamie stared at him in disbelief. "There has got to be some way we can find a compromise," she said tightly, trying to keep the desperation out of her voice. "You can't possibly expect me to just throw away four years of work like this."

"I don't make compromises," he said flatly. "I make laws."

"My God," Jamie exploded, "this isn't some little Central American country where you can just move in and set yourself up as dictator!"

"As far as this site is concerned, Irish, that's exactly who I am."

"Then I'll go over your head. I'll go right up to the president of the company if I have to, but I *will* get permission to finish this study at the dump."

He shrugged, seemingly unperturbed by her threat. "Go right ahead. I'll give you a list of the board of directors, if it'll help." He smiled then, a friendly little smile that made Jamie's heart drop. "I've got eighteen months to finish building this dam, Irish. And I can guaran-damn-tee you that I can stall you—and the president himself, if need be—long enough for me to do just that."

"It'll be too late in eighteen months!" Half-sick with frustration, Jamie gestured angrily toward a huge drawing tacked up on the wall. It was an artist's rendition of what the dam would look like when completed. Behind it, serene and dotted with fishermen and cruise boats, the newly created lake filled the valley. "Eighteen months from now the whole valley will be under water and my bears will be God knows where! That's the whole point of this study—to observe them while the water's rising and their territory is shrinking, to catch them right at the crisis point. In a year and a half, they'll have adapted—or moved on."

For a moment or two, Jamie actually thought he was going to waver. A thoughtful frown lodged between his brows as he stared at her, idly rubbing his chin with a scarred thumb. She could hear the rasp of late-day stubble against his nail, the sound distractingly erotic in the humid afternoon heat, and she found her gaze idly following the movement of his thumb as he traced the full, almost lush outline of his lower lip. The movement became slower, almost hypnotic, and Jamie suddenly realized he was watching her, his eyes smoky, almost hooded.

For a heartbeat of time their eyes locked, and in that small eternity Jamie knew exactly what he'd been thinking, knew she'd been thinking the same thing without even being aware of it. Knew without even knowing how she knew that she'd been naked in his mind, that his mouth had been hot and urgent on hers, that their bodies had been meshed so deeply and perfectly that they'd been a single entity.

The security guard, forgotten, shifted heavily and sighed. Slate visibly started, his gaze flickering toward the guard for the microsecond it took the spell to break. Jamie, feeling as though every bone in her body had just turned to gelatin, turned away and walked to the window.

"Uh...Mr. McCall...like, it's getting late and...uh... well, like, I'm supposed to be relieving Gerhardt at the gate...."

"What?"

Slate's voice was slightly hoarse and Jamie wondered if it was possible that he felt even half as shaken as she did. Probably not. He'd undoubtedly done it on purpose just to rattle her. And, Lord, he'd done a first-class job. It was going to take her a week just to remember her own name!

The security guard repeated his request and Slate said, "Yeah, go ahead. I'll escort Miss Kilpatrick to the gate myself."

"No!" She said it so anxiously that both men looked at her in surprise, and to Jamie's annoyance she felt herself blushing furiously. "I mean...there's no need. Unless—"

"No *unless*," he interrupted, the frown between his brows deeper now. He looked unsettled and a bit annoyed, and Jamie realized with a shock that whatever had happened between them just then hadn't been deliberate at all. And Slater McCall, dam builder *extraordinaire*, wasn't happy about it at all.

It made her hesitate, torn between pushing what might be an advantage and leaving while the leaving was good. "McCall..."

"No."

He said it so matter-of-factly that an instinctive tingle of anger shot through her, evaporating her embarrassment. "Damn you," she said with quiet venom, "you're just doing this to pay me back for the other night." The security guard, who had been standing impatiently by the door, looked suddenly attentive. Jamie ignored him. "Well, listen up, Slater McCall. I'll stay off your site—and you stay the hell off my mountain. Because next time, you just might not make it off alive!"

"You old devil! Haven't lost your touch, I see." A long, lean shadow figure materialized at the door of Slate's trailer where eddies of dust still marked Jamie's tempestuous exit. David Brubaker strolled across and poured himself a cup of Slate's coffee, then dropped into one of the chairs, and arranged his gangly length comfortably. "*That*, ol' buddy, is one spectacular lookin' lady. She's had every man on the site walking into walls ever since she turned up a couple of months ago. Many have tried, all have failed." He grinned broadly. "Then along comes Killer McCall and the rest is history."

Slate gave a snort. "I'd be history if she had her way." Briefly he told Dave the story, omitting that incendiary few seconds near the end when Jamie's eyes had met his and the universe had exploded. How the hell it had happened, he had no idea. In fact he wasn't even too sure *what* had happened, except that at one moment he was contemplating bears and biologists and the next he was indulging in the kind of erotic fantasy that could get a man into serious trouble should mind reading ever get popular.

And that's exactly what had happened. Those cat-tilted emerald eyes had met his full on and she'd known *exactly* what he'd been thinking, right down to the last intimate detail. And for that incredible breath-held instant she'd been right there in his mind with him and it had been as though they'd been making love then and there without either of them moving an inch. It was a wonder the whole trailer hadn't gone up in flames.

He came to after a moment, and realized that Dave was watching him with a small smile. "You in here for a reason, Brubaker, or just trying to waste my time?"

Dave's eyes twinkled, but all he said was, "Just thought I'd look in and make sure none of those death threats I've heard going around with your name attached has succeeded yet."

Slate smiled faintly. "That bad."

Dave shrugged. "Whoever took over from Cornelius was going to be mighty unpopular for a while." He took a cautious sip of the coffee, squinting at Slate through the steam. "Most men couldn't get away with what you're doing. You can. You've got a reputation for being one miserable son of a gun, but people know you're fair. A man will put up with a lot if he knows you're not asking him to do anything you're not willing to do yourself."

It was, Slate knew, the nearest thing to a compliment that Dave would give anyone. He smiled his thanks. "How's it going out there?"

"Things are getting done. It's starting to look more like a construction site than a three-ring circus. You can feel the change in the air—they've got the excitement back. You can even see it in the first-timers; suddenly they feel like they're part of something, like they're really doing something that matters. You gave them their pride back, buddy.''

Slate nodded, knowing what Dave meant. On every big project a special *esprit de corps* grew up among the workers: the dam suddenly became *their* dam, and bringing the job in on time and on budget wasn't just a goal, it was a point of pride with everyone involved. It was the sort of pride that made a welder take special pains to smooth a joint or a carpenter align his nail heads just so even when they knew that in six months their handiwork would be under a hundred feet of cold black water and no human eye would ever see the care they'd taken. It was that pride he deliberately counted on to get this job in on time, too: those five hundred men and women out there would do what he wanted done not for him, but for that sleek, curving wall of concrete rising above them.

Dave stretched and yawned vastly. ''Mind you, if these double shifts don't end soon, it's going to be a close call as to who's going to kill you first—me or Melanie.''

Slate feigned a look of shock. ''Don't tell me the happiest marriage in the western hemisphere's in trouble.''

''Marriage is fine,'' Dave grunted, ''it's the romance that's shot to hell. You may not have any love life to speak of, my friend, but I do. At least, I did. I don't mind working two shifts back-to-back, but when a man's too tired to make love to his wife for a week or more at a time...'' He let it trail off, shaking his head.

For some reason, Dave's teasing complaint irritated Slate unreasonably. He had his mouth half-open to remind Dave he was damned lucky to have a wife who'd put up with him at all before he realized how ridiculous it sounded. Or maybe it was just Dave's gibe about his not having a love life to suffer from the punishing schedule he was setting for everyone. Not having a permanent woman in his life had never bothered him before, even though it seemed to be a constant source of amusement to Dave. Why was he so touchy all of a sudden?

"Speaking of which," Dave said, as though reading Slate's mind, "you and that redheaded biologist got something going?"

Again, Slate felt a jolt of annoyance. Fought it down. "Open warfare," he said lightly. "The only woman I've got something going with these days is that dam out there. No time for anything else."

Dave looked at Slate for a long moment, his eyes uncharacteristically serious. "You know, old buddy, I think Melanie's right when she says it isn't healthy, a man of your considerable years spending as much time alone as you do. She says if you're not careful you're going to turn into one of those strange old coots who prefers dams to people and wanders around talking to himself."

"I do that already," Slate said equably. "Talk to myself, I mean. And as for strange—well, why a bright, pretty woman like Melanie would marry you is mighty strange in itself."

Dave laughed, unperturbed. "I'll tell you, Slate, if I'd known marriage was this great I'd have done it years ago."

As his old friend smiled into his coffee, Slate found himself fighting down something that felt suspiciously like envy. In spite of sounding like a newlywed, Dave had been married for close to five years now. He and Melanie had met in a tiny town much like Pine Lake and had swiftly and seemingly effortlessly fallen in love.

They'd gotten married just as the project that had brought Dave there was winding down, and Slate remembered how the entire crew—nearly a hundred and fifty hard-muscled, no-nonsense dam builders—had put on their best clothes and had stood in respectful silence in the little church as Dave Brubaker's new bride had walked down the aisle to marry one of their own.

Standing up as best man, Slate also remembered thinking to himself that it would never last. Because they didn't usually. He'd seen men time and time again fall into the same trap he'd once fallen into himself. Being an itinerant construction worker was a lonely, hard life and it was all too easy to slip under the coaxing spell of a pretty woman's smile. It was a fantasy they all had at one time or another—the dream of living "normal" lives complete with white picket fences and station wagons filled with chattering children and a loving, gentle woman at your side night after night.

He'd found himself dreaming it more than once. But the cold reality was that the David Brubakers and Slate McCalls and all the others out there weren't the kind of men for whom the dream would work. There was something within them that kept them on the move, some restlessness of spirit that drove them to forever seek what couldn't be found. In centuries past they'd been the explorers, the adventurers. In this century they were the astronauts and race-car drivers, the fighter pilots and deep-sea divers—and the engineers and architects and laborers who traveled the globe building things that all odds said couldn't be built.

"...around for supper one of these nights."

"What?" Slate looked at Dave blankly.

"I said," Dave repeated dryly, "that Melanie has been complaining that you've only been around once since you got on-site. She's beginning to think you're—"

"—I know, I know," Slate interrupted with a laugh, "turning into a hermit. Tell her the only reason I haven't been around is that it's difficult for me to control myself when I'm near her. If she can get rid of you for a couple of hours..."

"Like hell," Dave growled companionably. "You had your chance and turned it down, ol' buddy. No use complaining just because the man in second place turned up the winner."

"You were never in second place with Melanie," Slate assured him quietly. "She thought I was pretty hot stuff, but the minute you turned up at that town dance, she forgot I was even there. I could feel the electricity right across the room."

Dave grinned with pleasure, and Slate sighed inwardly, feeling inexplicably gloomy for no reason he could fathom. Dave and Melanie were so obviously in love it was almost painful to watch, and now that they had a baby son it was even worse. Every time he was with them he experienced the same tightness in his chest, the hard knot in his belly he was just starting to admit was jealousy.

Which was crazy. How could a man be jealous of his best friend's happiness? The holes in his own life that Dave's happiness seemed to underscore were ones he'd come to terms with long ago. He wasn't the marrying kind, he'd already realized that. Three years of marital warfare with Alison had proved it, and in the years since his divorce he'd put all those silly dreams to rest and had faced the reality that in choosing one way of life he'd forfeited another.

And that's just the way it was.

Four

———

I wouldn't waste any time if I were you," Terry Senkowski urged, his arms full of bear. "You cut way back on the dosage this time."

"It keeps catching on something!" Jamie frowned as she struggled to slip the thick fiberglass radio collar around the neck of the drugged black bear lying between them. "Got it!" Nodding in satisfaction as the two ends of the collar met, she slipped a bolt through the first pair of holes and started tightening the nut with swift, sure fingers. The bear wheezed noisily, tongue lolling. Its eyes were open and it tried to focus blearily on Jamie as she fumbled with the collar.

"Jamie, I'm telling you this thing is coming around!"

Terry sounded nervous, and Jamie nodded, feeling her own pulse quicken. It was easy to forget that she wasn't working with a teddy bear but with one of the most powerful, dangerous animals in the mountains. It was sprawled on its back, furry paws folded across its chest, its broad bear face sweetly appealing. But she had no illusions. Those paws were tipped with curved claws that could tear a tree apart, and the three-inch incisor teeth glistening in the sun could bring down a small elk. And behind those small brown eyes, bleary from the drugs now, was a shrewd, predatory intelligence.

The bear was definitely trying to focus its eyes and it moaned softly, the muscles in its throat working. The nut slipped from Jamie's fingers and she swore under her breath, trying to find it in the bear's thick, glossy pelt. Flies buzzed around them and Jamie shook her head to drive them off. One clawed foot lifted and pawed weakly at the air and the animal's sides gave a convulsive heave.

"Jamie!"

"Almost." The bear's breath was hot against her cheek as she bent her head nearer, trying to line the last two holes up. "Damn, it just won't—there!" She slipped the bolt through and started spinning the nut home. The bear took another deep, convulsive breath and lifted its head slightly, and Jamie, dashing sweat from her eyes with her forearm, could hear Terry swallow. "Just hang on to him—we've got another minute or so."

It was a magnificent young male, two years old at the most, and in beautiful condition considering how early in the season it was. He'd been in hibernation up until maybe six weeks ago, his body living off its own store of fat, but in the weeks that he'd been up and around he'd certainly done well for himself.

At the dump, Jamie reminded herself angrily. She hated to see one of these beautiful creatures reduced to rummaging through man's refuse, even though she knew that the bears loved it. They were such greedy, lazy things that a garbage dump must seem like a dream come true—instant catering. And with the most marvelous things: peanut butter and tuna-fish sandwiches and chocolate cake. In spite of her annoyance, she had to smile again, tightening the last nut with her fingers and reaching for the wrench. Just like kids, they'd prefer junk food to something nutritious any day. Especially when they didn't have to do anything more energetic to get it than rip open a plastic bag.

"Look out!"

Jamie ducked just as the bear wrenched its big head out of Terry's hands. Its snout and gleaming teeth missed Jamie's cheek by inches and then it collapsed again with a whistling groan.

Terry, wide-eyed with fright, knelt across the animal's thick neck. "Jamie, you've run out of time!"

The bear was giving eerie little moaning grunts now, and its jaws worked as it swallowed weakly, teeth clicking together with a wet, dangerous sound. "If I don't get these nuts tightened down," Jamie said through gritted teeth, "this collar won't stay on a season."

"And if you're dead," a gruff, impatient voice said from behind her, "it's not going to make a hell of a difference."

Jamie peered up through a tangle of her own hair, trying to see who the newcomer was, but all she could see were long male legs and a pair of muddy construction boots. The legs moved around to her left and straddled the bear, and in the next instant none other than Slate McCall eased his weight down over the bear's hind-quarters, pinning it to the ground.

"You!" Jamie nearly lost her grip on the wrench. Then the bear gave a groggy growl and reminded her that in about another minute the rest of the tranquilizer was going to wear off and they were going to have a couple of hundred pounds of irate Ursus Americanus on their hands. "What are you doing here?" she demanded as she secured the wrench over the last nut.

"Trying to keep you from getting eaten alive at the moment," he said, his fists tightening in the bear's fur as it made a convulsive attempt to throw his weight off.

"Finished." Jamie tossed the wrench into her tool kit and scrambled to her feet. "Let him go... and get back!"

Slate and her young assistant didn't need any urging. They were both on their feet and headed for the battered pickup truck under the trees before the bear even realized it was free. Jamie followed at a slower pace, watching the young bear anxiously as it made two futile attempts to get to its feet. It tried again and managed to get all the way up, then stood weaving gently from side to side, peering around nearsightedly.

"Jamie, will you get in the truck!"

The bear spotted Jamie just then. It lifted its head, snout wriggling energetically to catch her scent. Half-expecting it, Jamie wasn't surprised when the bear started to charge. It galumphed clumsily toward her, still too groggy to pick up much speed, but Jamie prudently retreated and hopped nimbly into the truck cab beside Slate.

"It's going after the tool box!"

Jamie groaned as the young bear spotted the tool box lying open on the ground and pounced on it. The bear picked the box up in its mouth and flung it rapidly from side to side, spraying tools in all directions, then dropped it and gave a buck, bringing both front feet down on the box. It did this again and again, growling and snorting, pausing now and again to snap at the other equipment lying around.

"Quite a temper," Slate said. "Do they react like this all the time?"

"Once in a while. They've got pretty short fuses—a tantrum like this isn't unusual. I watched one smash a rotten log to sawdust once because the mouse it had been trying to catch got away. It just went totally berserk for no reason other than the fact that it hadn't gotten its own way."

Slate grunted and leaned forward to peer over her shoulder at the bear. His breath tickled her ear and Jamie suddenly became conscious of just how close he was sitting, so close that she could feel his body heat against her back, the touch of his knee on her thigh, the pressure of his arm along hers where he'd braced his on the back of the truck seat to lean over to look out the side window.

She pulled her arm away as though she'd been scalded, and then immediately felt like an idiot. The man was hardly making a pass at her! In fact he was clearly more interested in the bear than he was in her, seemingly captivated by its almost childlike display of anger as it rampaged around the meadow smashing and mauling everything it could get its paws on. It pounced on Terry's denim jacket and started worrying it furiously, and she couldn't help but smile at Terry's groan of dismay, trying to ignore the steady pressure of Slate's hard thigh along hers as he shifted to get a better view.

He laughed, a deep relaxed rumble of sound that seemed to wrap itself comfortably around her. She tried not to start when he leaned forward again so his chest was pressed against her arm and shoulder. Her heart seemed to be having trouble beating and she wondered if he could hear it fluttering. She had to catch her breath when he laughed again at the bear's antics and his warm, moist breath curled around her ear like the sly touch of a lover's tongue.

Oh, God, she had to get out! She snatched for the door handle, caught herself in time. The three of them were shoehorned into the cab of the truck like sardines, and short of taking her chances with the bear there wasn't a lot she could do.

Slate seemed to lean even nearer, enveloping her in his body heat, his scent. Terry was exclaiming loudly about the fate of his jacket, but she hardly heard it; she was starting to feel suffocated and disoriented. Slate's powerful presence, alive and vital and explicitly male, seemed to fill the cab and Jamie suddenly felt so dizzy she had to close her eyes.

"Are you all right?" A large, warm hand clamped over her shoulder, bringing her back to reality. Jamie opened her eyes, faintly surprised to see they were still sitting in the truck in a mountain meadow, watching a bad-tempered bear vent its frustrations on what was left of Terry's jacket. She nodded, not daring to look at Slate, and pretended to watch the bear.

Slate took a deep breath, mildly annoyed to realize his heart was beating faster than it needed to. The clean unperfumed scent of Jamie's hair filled his nostrils and he clenched his teeth so hard they ached, wondering what in the hell was happening to him.

No, not just to him. He'd sensed the change in Jamie at the same instant, that moment in time when they'd both forgotten the bear and had become aware only of each other. He'd felt her stiffen slightly, heard the slight change in her breathing, had felt his own breathing slow and deepen in response.

He found himself unable to take his eyes off the silken curve of her throat, knowing he wanted to lower his mouth to that delicate hollow just under her ear as badly as she wanted him to. Her skin would be moist and slightly salty and she'd give a tiny start when he touched her with his tongue. He'd run a trail of tiny, light kisses to her hairline, then along the back of her neck, luxuriating in the surge of desire that would sweep through him as she moved against him, wanting him, aching for the touch of his hands, his mouth, his body.

He wanted to slip his arms around her and run his hands up the swell of her rib cage to the heavier swell of her breasts, knowing exactly the soft little indrawn breath she'd take when he slid the buttons on her shirt open and reached inside. She'd arch her back and his hands would be filled with her, then she'd whisper his name and he'd tug the shirt free of her jeans, and slowly, slowly draw the zipper down.

There'd be a moment of doubt, of hesitation, when his palm caressed the slight feminine curve of her stomach, but only a moment, then there would be that magical instant of trusting surrender when she'd relax the muscles of her thighs and he'd slip his hand lower, touching her.

She'd be like silk and butter and she'd tremble when he caressed her until the last of her shyness gave way and she opened herself to him completely. There'd be another moment or two of awkwardness, of shyness, then they'd be naked and in each other's arms and he'd ease himself into the honeyed warmth of her so gently and perfectly that she'd give a sigh of pleasure, and then those grass-green eyes would grow soft and smoky and she'd wrap those long slender legs around him and just let herself go....

"D'ya think it's safe to go out now?"

Terry's voice slammed Slate back into reality so hard he swore aloud, feeling as if he'd just been hit by a freight train. Dazed, he realized the little bear had ambled into the forest, anger apparently worked off.

He also realized his hand was still cupping Jamie's shoulder and that his mouth was a hairbreadth from her ear. He could see the sheen of moisture along her upper lip, a faint spray of golden freckles across the bridge of her nose. She was lightly flushed, and it was only then that he realized that sometime during that dreamlike interlude he'd meshed the fingers of his other hand with hers and her fingers had tightened on his with an almost desperate fierceness.

So she *had* felt it! Whatever "it" was. He'd never thought about the alchemy behind it enough to give it a name. He just knew that now it made him feel as though he'd been swept away on the crest of a flood-raging river. And that he wasn't entirely sure he liked it. Or maybe, he reminded himself thoughtfully as he looked down at Jamie, that was just because a man like him wasn't used to meeting something that couldn't be harnessed and controlled.

"Are you all right?" he murmured, the words this time having a whole other level of meaning.

"I'm...all right." Her voice was an unsteady whisper.

Her fingers were still clamped tightly around his and he tightened his for a reassuring moment, then slipped his hand free. He was painfully and urgently aroused and he gritted his teeth as he turned away from Jamie and rearranged his legs around the gearshift lever, concurrently cursing and blessing the tight-fitting jeans that both concealed and aggravated his condition.

God, how long had it been since he'd been put through this agony? Twenty years? Longer? It wasn't any less painful than he remembered, and for a moment he almost laughed aloud at how ridiculous it was. Men of thirty-seven didn't get this worked up over a bit of adolescent fantasizing. Men of thirty-seven didn't get this worked up over the real thing—not unless the situation was far enough along for the outcome to be pretty much a foregone conclusion, at any rate. And cold showers, if he remembered correctly, didn't work one damned bit.

"I think it's gone." Terry sounded slightly bewildered, not understanding what all the delay was.

Jamie, keeping her face turned so Slate couldn't see it, reached down for the door handle and pulled it. "Let's get this mess cleaned up," she said hoarsely, stepping out of the truck.

Terry opened the door on his side and slid out. Slate, who didn't relish the idea of trying to walk for the next few minutes, stayed where he was and looked down at Jamie. "You sure it's safe out there?"

It must have taken tremendous willpower, but Jamie met his gaze squarely, her eyes almost daring him to say or do even the slightest thing to acknowledge whatever had happened between them. "He's suffering from the world's worst hangover, Mr. McCall. He's gone to sleep it off—he won't be back."

"Irish," he said very quietly. "I think it's time you started calling me 'Slate.' All . . . considered."

There was a flicker deep in her eyes that Slate could have sworn was almost apprehension. Then it vanished. "If you wish," she said stiffly, looking so prim and proper that it took all of *his* willpower to stop himself from reaching down and taking her face between his hands and kissing her as she'd never been kissed before.

She must have seen a hint of it in his eyes, because hers widened ever so slightly. Then, as a warm blush spilled across her cheeks, she turned and nearly ran across to where Terry was picking up the muddy rags that had once been his denim jacket.

Oh, Lord. What was he doing? You never got involved with the local women, that was McCall Rule Number One. Women had the unsettling habit of falling in love when you least expected it, of taking things like white picket fences and babies for granted. He was too old to start pretending any of that could be his now. So what the hell was going on?

What, Jamie asked herself with a frown, was going on? She had no idea at all of how it had happened, but she was riding in Slate McCall's bright orange Monolith pickup truck while Terry drove *her* truck—the battered relic they used when working with bears because it provided better protection than her Jeep—back to Pine Lake. It had got all very confusing, trying to divide three people and a day's worth of research equipment between two trucks, but they'd done it. So now Terry was going back to his boarding house for the night, and she was going back to her cabin. With Slate McCall.

She slipped him a curious glance. Looking at his strong, even-featured profile, she couldn't help wondering what was going on under that head of tousled toast-brown hair. He didn't seem to be thinking about anything at all beyond getting his truck up this narrow, rutted road in one piece. He'd put it into four-wheel drive nearly a mile back, and they were still climbing.

"He seems like a nice kid."

She frowned, then realized he was talking about Terry. "He's taking biology at the University of Washington and is up here helping me for the summer as part of his field credit. Poor kid. I don't think they told him what he'd be doing."

Slate smiled, strong-arming the truck through a set of cross ruts that nearly wrenched the wheel from his hands. They were good hands, Jamie couldn't help noticing. Her father had hands like that, strong and square and competent. Yet gentle, too. She thought of Slate's hand slipping over hers that afternoon, of how natural it had been for her to braid her fingers with his, of the pressure of his other hand on her shoulder. He'd cradled her in the curve of his body as a man would a lover, and she'd fit there as though made for him alone.

And that was what scared her most of all.

There are two kinds of men in this world, her mother always said. *The safe kind, the kind who'll settle down and give you the secure, stable life a woman wants—and the dangerous kind, the kind who'll send your heart spinning with one reckless smile and twirl you off your feet and into a life you'll eventually regret.*

Her father had been one of the dangerous ones. He'd stolen her mother's heart and had carried her off into the wilderness like a conquering hero his prize. And her mother, once the novelty of being in love had worn thin, had loathed every minute of it, growing to resent and then hate the very man she'd once adored.

And I do not *want that happening to you, Jamie,* she'd said time and time again. *Marry a safe man, honey. They may not make your heart do handsprings every time they look at you, but in the long run you'll be happier.*

Frowning slightly, she glanced at Slate just at the instant he turned to look at her. And as their eyes met he gave her that lazy, warm smile that seemed to melt every bone in her body, and in that instant she knew she'd been right about him from the first moment they'd met: Slater Jordan McCall was probably the most dangerous kind of man of all.

She was still contemplating this when they reached her cabin. Slate helped her put away the equipment with a minimum of fuss and conversation, and when they were finished, Jamie stood on the wide, roofed veranda of the cabin awkwardly, wondering what she should do. The normal thing—the *polite* thing—would be to invite him in. But the last thing she wanted was this tall, wolf-eyed man prowling around her cabin. The last thing in the world.

She looked, Slate thought with amusement, like a nervous teenager on her first date.

He didn't really know why he'd come up here with her, apart from idle curiosity. He looked up at the cabin. It was considerably larger than he'd expected, and he let his gaze run over it assessingly, taking in the expert fit of the logs, the slope of the roof, the way it was tucked against a sheltering ridge of rock with its back to the prevailing winds.

Nice. He nodded to himself, admiring it as one expert admires the work of another. Turning, he found himself admiring the builder even more: he could not possibly have chosen a more spectacular view. The valley was at its widest here, green cloaked and serene in the late afternoon sun. Gushing through it, as clear as green glass, the river tumbled its icy mountain water over the rocks and stones of the wide gravel bed. Raising his eyes, Slate gazed up at the rampart of forbidding, wolf-toothed peaks serrating the sky above him. The snows on their upper slopes gleamed gold and bloodred in the lowering sun, and even this far down the wind smelled of ice.

He suddenly realized that Jamie had come over to stand beside him, her face thoughtful as she gazed out across the valley. "It's spectacular," he said quietly. "Whoever built this place knew what he was doing."

"My father built it."

"Well, if your dad ever wants a job, Irish, tell him to look me up."

"He died a little over a year ago," she said softly.

Even the late afternoon shadows couldn't hide the pain in her eyes, and Slate cursed himself soundly. "I'm sorry."

She smiled faintly. "It was a massive stroke—quick and painless, the doctor said. He was standing out here when it happened. He used to come out every morning and watch the sun touch the peaks and work its way down. He said it made his day go easier, knowing there could be such beauty in the world. I keep thinking that he died very, very happy."

"He sounds like a remarkable person."

"He was."

His daughter is remarkable too, Slate nearly said aloud, catching himself just in time. She was a never-ending surprise, this odd, green-eyed woman, and about as easy to pin down as river mist. Every time he met her she was a completely different person; it could keep a man seriously off balance just trying to keep up with her.

"Aren't you ever lonely up here all by yourself?"

"Lonely?" Slate had never noticed what a musical laugh she had. "How could I be lonely surrounded by all this?" Her graceful gesture took in the entire valley. "I feel safe up here. Protected." She looked at the mountains across the valley, the tall barricade between them and civilization. "It's out there that I feel alone and . . . lonely sometimes. Almost as though I'm not really a part of their world at all." Her voice was soft and for a moment Slate got the feeling she'd forgotten he was even there.

She was so touchingly vulnerable that he very nearly put his arm around her before he caught himself. Damn it, what *was* it about this woman that kept catching him off guard like that? He realized suddenly that he was cold. The sun had dropped swiftly, leaving the valley in shadow, and the wind had an edge to it that cut right through his heavy wool work shirt. Jamie must have felt it, too; she shivered suddenly, and they turned without speaking and started back up to the cabin.

Jamie paused at the bottom of the steps to the veranda, looking uncertain. Deliberately giving her time, Slate braced one foot on the front bumper of the truck and pretended to tighten his bootlace.

"Would you . . . that is, I could make coffee. If you wanted."

Her eyes were filled with apprehension, the invitation already regretted, and for a moment he nearly did the honorable thing and declined. But he was reluctant to leave. He wanted to see the inside of the cabin, for one thing, as he was strangely curious about the humdrum intimacies of her life. And besides, he rationalized, he still hadn't talked to her about the bears.

"I wouldn't mind a cup," he said easily, amused to see the apprehension in her eyes turn to outright nervousness. *Relax, Jamie,* he wanted to tell her. *We're both adults. Nothing's going to happen that we don't both want to happen.* But he left it unsaid, knowing that far from reassuring her it would probably send her running.

Five

Jamie nodded unhappily. She walked up the steps and pulled the door open and Timber bounced out in a frenzy of ecstatic barking, eyes dancing with delight. Then he spotted Slate and froze, bristling and businesslike, until Jamie patted his broad head. "It's all right, Timber."

It was, obviously, the magic phrase. In the next instant he was all exuberant energy and doggy smiles again, wriggling and prancing with excitement, his big tail windmilling. He wrapped a long wet tongue around Slate's extended fingers in way of greeting, then galloped energetically into the kitchen where Jamie was already opening a tin of food.

She grinned at Slate. "Some watchdog, huh!"

Slate laughed. "He's my friend for just as long as you are. Get you upset, and I'll probably lose a leg."

She gave him an amused look. "I guess that's an incentive to behave yourself, Mr. McCall."

"Believe me, Ms. Kilpatrick," he said dryly, "I never intended to do otherwise."

She gave him a quick look, as though not too sure of just how serious he was, then carried the bowl of food out onto the veranda. Timber bounded after her and while she was occupied filling his water bowl, Slate looked around him.

Just what he'd expected to find, he had no idea, but it certainly wasn't *this*. The place looked like a luxury ski lodge at Tahoe. It was huge, made up of a series of cunningly contrived nooks and angles that visually divided the one big room into smaller living spaces. A large kitchen took up most of one end, an island counter separating it from a big dining room, which in turn overlooked the sunken living room. A fieldstone fireplace the size of a small mountain jutted out across one end, creating a half wall behind which Slate caught a glimpse of a bed and pine dresser.

It was filled with a comfortable clutter of solid, inviting chairs and sofas, tables holding lamps and framed photographs, and a couple of overstuffed hassocks. The walls were hung with paintings, a couple of racks of deer antlers, shelves of ornaments and all the other bits and pieces of treasure that one collects over a lifetime. The whole place was imbued with a subtle but uncompromising masculinity, the kind of place where a man could put his feet up and be truly at home, surrounded by his books, his dogs and his memories.

"Quite a place," Slate said dryly as Jamie came back in. "I was expecting something a bit more . . . Spartan."

She smiled as she started measuring coffee into the percolator. "Dad liked roughing it in comfort. He put in running water, electricity—a generator, actually. He wanted a fridge for his ice cream." Her smile widened. "He loved ice cream."

Slate strolled down into the living room. A glass-fronted display case held a collection of arrowheads and stone axes, another one, rocks and crystals, all meticulously labeled. "What did your father do?"

"Geologist. He worked with various mining and oil companies over the years, as well as doing a lot of government work—looking for uranium, mainly. He even worked on a dam once. The Manicouagan, up in northern Quebec.''

"Before my time." Slate smiled as she joined him. "But it was a landmark engineering project. People still talk about it.''

"It impressed the daylights out of my dad," she said with a quiet laugh. "He had a soft spot for dams ever after. I think that's why he didn't fight yours very seriously.''

"Meaning that if he had, we wouldn't be here?''

"People around here looked up to my dad," she said simply. "They called him The Prof because he was the only man in three hundred miles with a college degree." She smiled the same sad smile he'd seen before. "He was quite an engineer in his own way. He was always inventing something or other—he even designed a solar-heated water system so he could take a bath without having to heat the water on the stove. Only problem is," she added with a chuckle, "it rains so much up here the water's only lukewarm half the time. After he put the generator in, he added an electric hot-water tank.''

"Did he design that trap you caught me in the other night?" he asked with deceptive nonchalance.

Bad move. The goodwill he'd managed to build up vanished in the time it took to say the words aloud, and she turned away, shoulders rigid. "I've been wrestling bears all day, so if you'll excuse me, I'm going to have a shower.''

She headed toward the bedroom without a backward glance, and a few minutes later Slate heard the sound of running water. He frowned and wandered over to the fireplace, stood staring into the empty grate. On a whim he knelt down and opened the mesh doors. Whatever mystery lay behind that trap, it didn't have anything to do with her bear studies, he was damned sure about that. Either her work with the bears was just an elaborate cover-up for whatever was really going on, or she was working for someone else on the side. But who? And on *what*?

He soon had a crackling fire going. Sitting on a large hassock beside the hearth, he luxuriated in this rare treat, smiling at his own self-indulgence. A man who enjoyed fireplaces, he reminded himself, shouldn't have a job that meant living in construction-camp trailers. His glance was drawn to the big easy chair pulled near the hearth. It had probably been her father's favorite, the arms worn through, the seat cushion permanently indented. There was an empty coffee cup sitting on the table beside it, a stack of books, an open notepad and a pen. A lap robe lay over the arm where it had been set aside, and a pair of small, pink slippers peeked out from underneath.

Slate smiled, visualizing her sitting here in the evenings with Timber sleeping at her feet, making notes of the day's work while surrounded by the things her father had loved. A man's pipe lay near the base of the reading lamp and he picked it up and turned it curiously in his fingers.

The percolator started bubbling and Slate was halfway to the kitchen when a laundry basket on the dining-room table caught his eye, and again he found himself smiling. He picked up the garment that lay on top of the neatly folded wool shirts and denim jeans, trying to equate *this* with the self-described bear wrestler in the other room. The filmy rose-pink bra was no more than cobwebs and lace, and Slate's grin widened as he held it up. Matching briefs lay under it, more cobwebs and a froth or two of pink lace and appliqués.

Well, well, well. There were, he decided with amusement, no end of surprises to the mysterious Jamie Kilpatrick.

"Do you mind!" A tanned hand snatched the lacy undergarments out of his fingers, and Slate found himself face-to-face with their annoyed owner. "A fetish for women's lingerie, McCall?"

"Nope," he replied with a broad grin. "Just indulging in some good old-fashioned fantasizing."

Cheeks burning, Jamie stuffed the offending garments under a pair of folded blue jeans and moved the entire basket out of Slate's reach. What in heaven's name had ever possessed her to buy those silly things in the first place?

She'd seen them on her last trip to Vancouver and had them paid for and wrapped up before she'd even stopped to wonder what she was doing. God knows what he was thinking.

"Just give it to me straight up, thanks."

Jamie stared at him, then realized he was talking about the coffee even though there was still a gleam of amusement in his eyes. He was leaning against the end of the counter, looking tall and relaxed and very much at home. Rugged and deeply tanned, he looked as though he should be making adventure movies in Hollywood instead of standing in her kitchen making her heart do decidedly strange things.

Flustered for no earthly reason, she turned around and started busying herself finding mugs and pouring coffee.

"Do you take cream?" he asked.

"No. I mean yes. It's—that is, I'll get it."

Slate pulled the fridge open and took out the cream. "You hungry, Irish?"

"Yes. I mean no! That is, I don't—"

Seemingly unfazed by her sudden inability to string two coherent words together, he perused the contents of the fridge thoughtfully. "You should be, wrestling bears all day. And I'm starved. You've got eggs in here. Sausages. Potatoes and...let's see...aha! Green onions." He looked around the door at her. "How about supper? You didn't have plans, did you?"

"I..." She had the lie half-formed before she realized he knew damned well that she didn't have a thing planned for tonight beyond a hot shower and a solitary evening in front of the fire.

"I'm cooking," Slate added, seeing her hesitate. "And I make great hash browns." He watched her waver, fighting temptation, then finally give in.

"You're awfully pushy, McCall," she muttered, retreating to the other side of the island with her coffee.

"It's 'Slate,' remember? And I'm not pushy. I'm hungry."

"Pushy," she corrected. "I have a feeling you're used to getting your own way."

"Guilty as charged," he admitted cheerfully, rummaging through the cupboards until he found a skillet. He tossed a wad of butter in it and set it on the stove, then started breaking eggs into a bowl.

"Which makes me wonder why you're up here." She took a sip of coffee, watching him cook over the rim of the mug. "That logging road where you found Terry and me today doesn't go anywhere."

He finished dicing onions, grinning lazily. "Maybe I was just out for a relaxing drive in the country."

"Maybe pigs can fly."

Slate laughed. "You're right—I was out looking for you." He glanced at her, serious now. "I need your help, Irish."

"*My* help?" She couldn't keep the surprise out of her voice.

"Kind of ironic, isn't it, considering I tossed you out on your very attractive backside a few days ago." He glanced at her again, found her watching him warily. "I don't make mistakes very often, Irish. In my position I don't get many second chances—decisions have to be made, and they usually have to be made fast. But when I do make a mistake, I own up to it and repair what damage I can. I've made two mistakes in the past week: I thought I could handle the bear problem myself, and I let a pretty face distract me from the fact that the lady behind it knows what she's talking about."

"You have a strange way of apologizing, McCall. If that's what you're doing."

"Hey, I do the best I can," he said with a laugh.

"I'm listening."

"We're having a hell of a time with the bears at the dump. And it's getting worse by the day. Used to be when the kitchen staff drove out with the garbage all they'd have to do was lean on the truck horn a few times and the bears would back right off. But now they treat it like a lunch bell. The driver blows the horn and he's got bears coming at him from all directions. Yesterday two guys got trapped there for over an hour—the bears swarmed over the truck like fleas on a dog. The kids inside were shaking for an hour afterward and they swear they'll quit before they'll take another truckload of garbage out there. I can't say as I blame them.''

"I told Cornelius two years ago that you were going to have serious trouble, and he just shrugged me off. As long as the bears know there's an easy source of food here, they're not going to move up-slope when the weather warms as they'd normally do. And each year the sows bring their cubs in, teaching them to be garbage bears, too. Last year's cubs don't know there's any other way of life, and this spring's litter is learning right alongside them. Next year you'll have that many more to worry about.''

"My men have started carrying guns,'' Slate said quietly.

"Guns?'' Her eyes widened in horror. "Slate, you can't—!''

"I had no choice, Jamie. I've given orders that the kitchen staff is to go out in threes—two to unload the garbage and one standing guard with a rifle.''

"If one of your men kills one of my bears, I'll—''

"Jamie, men's lives are at stake here!''

"And whose fault is that?'' She banged her coffee mug down and strode into the living room, back rigid with anger.

Swearing under his breath, Slate turned the heat down and went after her. "Jamie...''

"Why don't you just get out of here and leave me alone?''

"And why don't you quit being so damned hostile for five minutes, and help me come up with a solution?'' He felt his temper start to rise and struggled to fight it down.

"You've already got the solution you want,'' she snapped, eyes flashing. "Guns are always the ultimate solution.''

"Damn it, will you listen to me for a minute!'' He caught her shoulders and swung her around. "No one's going to be sorrier than I'll be if one of those bears gets shot out there, understand me? I hate waste—waste of any kind, but I especially hate seeing something killed just because it gets in the way. But we're not the only ones to blame. Seems to me you've been getting a hell of a lot of mileage out of that dump and the bears it's attracting." He released her so abruptly that she stumbled back a step or two. "Look, Jamie," he said with quiet intensity, "the two of us have gotten off to a bad start, but for God's sake, at least meet me halfway!"

He could tell just by her eyes that every instinct she possessed was screaming at her not to listen. She opened her mouth as though to tell him again to get out, then combed her thick hair back from her face with both hands. "Oh...hell," she whispered, turning away. She walked across to the wide hearth and sat down, elbows on knees, face cupped pensively in her hands. "You tried fencing them out."

"They walk through it like it isn't even there." He went over and sat on the hassock beside her. "It was suggested we burn it, but the reports say Cornelius tried that last year and it didn't work."

"They wound up with singed, mad bears," Jamie told him. "And a bunch of irate environmentalists threatening legal action over the smoke, not to mention the danger of forest fire. Then they tried burying it." She laughed, looking sidelong at Slate. "The bears used to line up along the edge of the dump, waiting for the cat operator to finish. Then they'd hustle in and dig it all up again—it got to be a game with them."

"Electric fence?"

She shook her head. "They don't even feel it through their fur. And if they *do* get a jolt they go nuts. Like that one today, only worse. There are repellents available. Smoke bombs, noisemakers. Problem is, bears are smart. A deterrent will work once, but usually only once. And," she added, straightening with a sigh, "that's only part of your problem."

"Part?" Slate felt his heart sink.

"Those bears out there depend on your dump as their major food supply—especially last year's cubs, who haven't learned to forage for themselves. If you cut them off cold, you're going to have a lot of very hungry, very bad-tempered bears on the prowl. Bears who have completely lost their fear of man. At least now they're more or less content to stay out there. Get rid of that food supply, and they're going to be swarming through your camp like the Vandals sacking Rome.''

Slate swore wearily, rubbing his chin. ''So you're telling me it's too late.''

''I'm just suggesting you come up with a plan to wean them slowly—cut back on the free food to give them time and incentive to find other sources. At the same time, find an alternative way to dispose of your garbage.'' She gave him a jocular smile. ''Not much of a challenge for a man who spends his life defying rivers.''

Slate lifted an eyebrow, but he merely smiled and stood up. ''Time to eat, Irish. You set the table, I'll finish cooking.''

''So, tell me. How did you wind up wrestling bears for a living?'' Full of sausages, scrambled eggs and half a bottle of surprisingly good wine that Jamie had unearthed in her father's liquor cabinet, Slate sprawled out in the big easy chair in front of the fire. The wine and the warmth of burning pine had made him sleepy and altogether too comfortable, and in spite of a little voice telling him to go home before he got any *more* comfortable, he was quite content to stay.

Jamie smiled. She was sitting on the floor, leaning against the hearth with her legs stretched out in front of her and crossed at the ankles, a glass of wine at her elbow. Timber dozed beside her, his big head in her lap. The firelight behind her made her hair look like flame itself, and Slate found his mind prone to wander off in all sorts of tantalizing directions unless he held it firmly in control.

''I was born in a survey camp in Alaska, and I grew up in construction camps and geological outposts from the Beaufort Sea to Frobisher Bay. If it was north of the sixtieth, I was probably there." She laughed quietly. "One thing there is *never* a shortage of up there is bears—black, cinnamon, brown, grizzly, polar. My dad believed that knowledge is the best antidote to any danger there is, so he learned everything he could about them. He passed it on to me. I was an expert by the time I was six. I just never outgrew my fascination with them."

"Your mother must have been some kind of special lady," Slate said quietly. A sudden memory of his own mother came to him then, just a child's hazy image of pale tumbling hair and a tinkling laugh. She'd left when he was five and he'd never seen her again, had memories beyond that only of other, faceless women, some who were pleasant, others less so, none memorable enough to have left even a name imprinted on his mind.

"She hated every minute of it," Jamie said just as quietly. She was silent for a while, absently stroking Timber's big ears. "Her father was dean of literature at Princeton, and she used to tell me how they'd spend their evenings with members of the faculty, drinking sherry and talking philosophy and art." She smiled again. "Mom was engaged to an English major when she met Dad and got swept off her feet. He was the son of a physics prof, and the most exciting, handsome man she'd ever seen." Jamie laughed softly. "Her words, not mine. A week later, she'd broken her engagement and had eloped with my father, and a month after *that* she was living in a log shack on Baffin Island. Dad had been offered a teaching position and Mom had thought he was going to take it, but at the last moment the call of the wild hit him and he backed out."

"And your mother found herself playing frontierswoman instead of the wife of a geology prof."

"Exactly." She looked down, running the dog's ears between her fingers. "I was born that first year. She was sure Dad would move back to civilization then, but of course he didn't. She stuck it out for another twelve years."

"Along about the time your mom realized you were growing into a real heartbreaker," Slate said with a chuckle, "and she'd soon have to be beating the construction workers and young geologists off with a stick."

Jamie gave a peal of laughter. "She caught me and Billy Jacobs in a drilling-core shed involved in what she described to my father as 'hanky-panky.'" She grinned. "It was all very innocent—how much mischief can two ten-year-old kids get into at twenty below zero? We still had our mitts on!"

"But it was enough to scare the hell out of your mother."

The laughter left Jamie's eyes. "She told Dad she wanted me to grow up like a normal teenager, and she gave him an ultimatum: her or the job. When he tried to explain he couldn't quit in the middle of a project, she moved to Vancouver and took me with her." Timber whimpered in his sleep and Jamie stroked his muzzle. "Dad came up here, and Mom divided her time between Vancouver and Boston, where her parents were."

"And you divided your time between here and Vancouver."

Jamie nodded, her face shadowed and pensive. "I hated it," she whispered, more to herself than to him. "It was like being two separate people. In Vancouver, I was my mother's perfect, well-mannered little daughter. Up here, I was Ben Kilpatrick's kid, the worst tomboy in the valley."

"And I bet I can guess which one you preferred," Slate said with a lazy laugh.

Her head shot up and she stared at him, mouth tightening. "I didn't prefer either one of them. I loved both my parents, McCall. I never took sides." Then, embarrassed by her outburst, she looked down at the dog, her cheeks flushed. "Sure I enjoyed spending my summers up here more than I did going to school in Vancouver. Any kid would."

Slate said nothing, puzzling over her reaction. Resentment at being forced to live in two worlds yet choose neither? Guilt at having secretly preferred living up here with the father she obviously adored, yet not risking her mother's anger—and perhaps withheld affection—by admitting it?

"Mom is still in Vancouver. She owns an art gallery there."

"And what does she think of her perfect, well-mannered daughter rolling around in the dirt wrestling with black bears?"

To Slate's relief, she laughed, wrinkling her nose expressively. "I'm the despair of her life! Of course, she hopes that when I'm—" She stopped short. Her face went very carefully expressionless, and she looked up at him politely. "And you, McCall? You've heard my entire life history, and I don't know any more about you than I did a week ago. Aside, of course, from the fact that you're a very talented cook."

When you're what? he was dying to ask, knowing damned well that if he did she'd close up like a clam. There were some secrets, obviously, that were impervious to firelight and wine.

He smiled down at her lazily, approving of the way fire and wine made her eyes sparkle, the slender backlit curve of her throat. She was wearing the inevitable pants, moss-green corduroy this time, but had replaced the businesslike denim shirt she'd had on that afternoon with a hunter-green sweater in a light wool that accented both eyes and figure to a degree that made his breath catch every now and again.

She'd kicked her shoes off sometime during the evening and he found himself gazing at her toes, each tipped in a delicate pink nail polish. Again, the dichotomy between this softly feminine woman and the hard-as-nails biologist he'd encountered previously amused him, and he caught himself thinking about those filmy pink undergarments in the laundry basket.

Which wasn't a wise idea. He wrenched his mind from its undisciplined course and concentrated instead on what she'd asked. "Nothing much to tell. I spent a childhood much like yours, growing up in construction camps around the world. Only difference is that it took my mother six years to leave instead of twelve—and she left for good. I had a lot of 'substitute mothers' after that." He smiled faintly. "I think my old man may have even married a couple of them. When I was finally old enough to leave home, I did. Stayed with an aunt and her family in Pennsylvania for a while, went to college, got a degree in civil engineering . . . and here I am.''

Her mouth curved at the corners. ''And you followed in your father's footsteps.''

''In the blood, I guess.''

''And . . . the women?'' She asked it almost too carelessly. ''I suppose you have a wife in every port, do you?''

''No.'' It sounded overly clipped, even to his own ears. He stared into the fire, feeling old angers, old regrets, trickle through him. He shook himself free and looked into Jamie's eyes, smiling. ''Before you get the wrong idea, I *do* like women. I got married right out of college—it lasted three years. Women and dams seem to be mutually exclusive. It's hard to give one all the attention it needs without neglecting the other.''

She nodded slowly. ''So you live the typical wanderer's life, do you, finding a little romance here, a little there?''

Slate held her gaze, smile broadening. ''I wish,'' he said dryly, ''that I could say you're wrong. But you're a big girl; I don't have to explain the facts of life to you. There have been a few romantic interludes in my life, in various places at various times. Nothing that lasted.'' He swallowed the last of the wine, meeting her eyes over the glass. ''How about you? Does the intrepid bear wrestler of Skookum Mountain have a man in her life?''

She looked down, frowning very slightly. ''As a matter of fact,'' she said quietly, ''she does.'' It took Slate so by surprise that he merely stared at her. Still frowning, she sighed and got to her feet. ''Coffee?''

''Fine,'' he managed as an afterthought. His own reaction annoyed him. Why did it come as such a surprise that she was involved with someone? She was attractive, bright, a delight to be with. Any man would be lucky to have her. Suddenly restless, he got up and tossed a log on the dying fire, then started wandering aimlessly.

There was a big desk and a file cabinet at the far e̟
the dining room. A survey map of the valley hung abov
long worktable covered with stacks of paper and book⹁,
confettied with multicolored pins, and a computer took up
most of the desk. A tower of stacking wire baskets sat on
one free corner, filled with newspaper clippings and bun-
dles of paper clipped together.

Idly, he picked one of the clippings up and scanned it,
surprised that it wasn't about bears—as he'd expected—but
a story about a nine-hundred-pound sturgeon that had been
found washed up on the shore of Seattle's Lake Washington over two years previously. There was a fuzzy photo of
the eleven-foot-long fish and Slate felt his skin crawl. There
were similar clippings attached, all about the same ninety-
year-old fish that scientists believed to be the source of long-
standing tales about a huge, duck-eating monster lurking in
the lake. Smiling, Slate tossed the collection of articles aside
and picked up another one.

This one detailed the adventures of two wilderness
campers in Oregon who swore they'd been stalked by a tall,
hair-covered creature they identified as bigfoot. There was
a blurry photo of something vaguely man shaped that was
undoubtedly a hungry bear looking for a handout.

Curious, Slate rifled through the top basket, finding
dozens more clippings detailing incidents involving bigfoot. Glancing at the nearby bookcase, he realized that they,
too, followed the bigfoot theme. One one shelf there was a
pile of photographs of the elusive animal, some original
prints, others that had been cut out of newspapers and
magazines, and Slate felt the spot between his shoulder
blades tingle. He picked up a pile of bound scientific research papers and reports, not surprised to see they were
about bigfoot, many of them with Ben Kilpatrick's name
listed either as author or consultant. Many of them were
field papers, some were manuscripts of articles that he'd
submitted to various scientific journals.

It was only then that he took a second look at the piece of
misshapen rock he'd taken for a paperweight. Looking at it

more closely he realized that it wasn't rock at all, but plaster—and that the reason it was misshapen was, quite simply, because it was the cast of a footprint. "What the hell...?"

There were others, some just rough indentations in the plaster that could have been almost anything, some perfectly detailed prints, right down to the skin whorls on the toes. But it was the complicated electronic display panel above the computer that finally caught Slate's attention and held it raptly. He'd seen enough like it in the control rooms of power plants to know it was a sophisticated alarm panel. It was linked to the computer and a small printer, and the longer he stood there staring at it, the stronger the tingle between his shoulder blades got. "Well, I'll be damned," he finally whispered. "*That's* what this is all about!"

Watching him from the kitchen, Jamie felt a wave of unease sweep over her. "Coffee's ready," she called in her cheeriest voice. "I'll take it down by the fire, and we can—"

He scarcely even looked at her. "Forget the coffee, Irish," he growled. "Come over here and explain all this to me."

She set the coffee things on a tray and started carrying it toward the living room, damned if she was going to pander to his curiosity. "Explain what? It's just a monitor system for... for my bears. It tracks the radio collars."

Slate's one word of disbelief was earthily profane, and Jamie felt a stab of anger. "Look, it's too complicated to explain easily. And frankly, I'm too tired to even try tonight, so—"

"Sweetheart," Slate said with silky calm, "I'm an engineer, remember? My specialty may be throwing dams across rivers, but I know a thing or two about computers—and alarm systems. Some part of this rig may very well monitor your bear collars, but I'm not interested in that. What I'm interested in is this network of pit traps you've got set up out there."

"Without putting too fine a point on it, McCall, it's none of your business."

"It's my business, Irish," he said in a hard, dangerous voice. "Considering you caught me in one of 'em the other night."

"Slate—"

"You're hunting bigfoot, aren't you? You're out to catch yourself an abominable snowman!"

Six

————

There wasn't much point in lying.

"They're called Sasquatch around here," she said quietly. She put the coffee down and walked over to join Slate. "Although Dr. Grover Krantz at Washington State has more or less officially named them *Gigantopithecus blacki*. Whatever you call them, my father spent over thirty years studying them—collecting data, authenticating sightings, correlating information gathered from all over the world. In the past few years he narrowed his search to central B.C. and Washington." She nodded at the map. "The blue pins are where footprints or other solid signs have been found, the red are positive sightings."

"The map's solid with them!"

"Skookum is an Indian word meaning evil genies or bogeymen," she said with a dry smile. "Legends of Sasquatch in the valley go back for hundreds of years."

The suggestion of a smirk lifted one corner of Slate's mouth. "Giant hairy apes."

A jolt of familiar anger seared Jamie. "An apt description of some men I know," she said with precision.

It didn't seem to faze him. "And you're going to catch one."

"McCall, this all may be perfectly hilarious to you, but a lot of solid, respected scientists believe it's possible. It was a dream of Dad's to prove that Sasquatch exist, but he died before he could do it."

"And you want to prove to the world that he was right."

"Something like that, I guess." She hesitated. "A lot of people thought he was crazy. My father was a brilliant man, but he ... well, he sometimes had a problem with drinking. Not often—he could go for months without even thinking about it. But once or twice a year he'd go into these black Irish moods and lock himself in here, just brooding and drinking. It didn't affect his work, but there are people who dismiss everything he did because of it."

"And you think these traps will work."

For the first time since he'd started grilling her, Jamie had to smile. "I caught you, didn't I?"

Slate's strong mouth tipped aside in a wry smile. "That you did," he murmured, his gaze capturing hers. "Although you never have said what you intend to do with me now you've got me."

There was such a wealth of possibilities in that seductive purr that Jamie's knees went a little weak. Her gaze went involuntarily to Slate's right temple, hidden now by a beguiling cowlick of golden-brown hair that simply begged to be run through her fingers. She reached up and brushed it back before she even realized what she was doing.

The scrape had healed cleanly although the skin around it was still faintly bruised. "I never have apologized for that, have I? I felt sick about it later—all I could see was you lying in that trap with a broken neck."

"It would have set the project back a week or two, all right," he chuckled. "Lucky I have a head like concrete."

The dam wouldn't be the only one suffering a loss, Jamie thought as those pale amber eyes held hers, seemingly drawing her toward them. Strange that she'd ever thought he had wolf eyes. They were much too gentle to be wolf's eyes, much too . . . close!

How he kept from taking her into his arms then and there Slate didn't know. Her eyes were so near, green depths faintly puzzled. And that mouth! Just a kiss away. Moist lips slightly parted as though anticipating the taste of his, the expression on her face as expectant and wondering as any child's.

Somehow, he managed to turn away. Stumbled by her as though sleepwalking, every cell in his body vibrating with a sudden need so strong it made his teeth ache. Walked to the door, making some excuse about the coffee.

Stepping out into the crisp mountain air, he was surprised to discover it was pitch black. He looked at his watch and was even more surprised to see it was well past eleven. They'd been sitting in there for hours, talking, laughing. . . .

Oh, God, McCall, what are you doing? He asked it silently, knowing the only answer he'd get was the one he didn't want to hear.

"Thank you for supper," she said almost shyly, coming out into the night to stand beside him. Timber ambled out behind them, yawning and stretching. "For the whole evening, in fact. I don't have . . . company often."

Male company, was what she'd been about to say. He smiled to himself and walked down the three steps resolutely, proud of his willpower. "Good night, Jamie."

"Good night."

He was halfway to the truck before he stopped. He stood there for a moment or two, then swore under his breath, turned on one heel, and strode back to the cabin.

She was still standing where he'd left her and she looked at him curiously. "Did you forget something?"

"You might say that." He took the steps in two long strides and she gazed up at him questioningly. "I'm probably going to regret doing this," he growled, "but I'll regret it even more if I don't." And with that he cupped her wind-cooled face in his hands and brought his mouth down over hers exactly as he'd been aching to do for the past five hours.

She gave a tiny, indrawn squeak of shock, every part of her going rigid. And then, as though some deep inner struggle had come to an end, she melted against him.

Her lips parted almost hesitantly and he slipped the tip of his tongue between them, half-crazy to taste her, to be so deep inside her he'd never be free again. She gave a shudder as he probed gently between her teeth, easing them apart, savoring the moist sweetness of her. The first touch of her tongue was so delicate it was scarcely there at all, withdrawn almost before it touched his, and he probed deeper, coaxing her, feeling the tension in her body as she fought this last remaining battle with herself.

And then it was over. Her tongue brushed his, lingered, met, entwined. Each thrust was a voluptuous symphony of silk and fire, want and need. She answered questions he hadn't even asked yet, letting him explore each secret part of her with slow, erotic enjoyment. As the kiss deepened, Slate felt a shaft of fire shoot through him, as hot and urgent as any volcanic core, and he groaned her name, his hands suddenly exploring the sweet curve of her back, drawing her against him.

She followed effortlessly and then her hands were on his shoulders, sliding up his neck and into his hair and she was pressed against him. He could feel the pressure of her breasts against his chest, the tantalizing softness at the juncture of her thighs as she moved against him, seeking him, finding him. He could no more have stopped the physical response of his body than he could have stopped an avalanche but even while half expecting her to pull away, he wasn't surprised when she instead moved subtly against him, bold yet touchingly shy as though not completely certain of his reaction.

He slid his palm down her back until it rested on the upper swell of her bottom and he pressed her against him, holding her there, his tongue moving on hers in slippery, slow rhythms more expressive than words. Her fingers flexed in his hair and she gave a shuddery moan, kissing him back with a slow, drugging intensity that nearly sent him that last, aching distance right then and there.

"Oh, Slate!" It was a breathless gasp as she wrenched her mouth from his. "My God, what are we doing?"

"What we've both been wanting to do since the night you pulled me out of that trap," Slate groaned against her mouth. He ran his mouth across her cheek, buried his face in the silken torrent of her hair. "What we've both been thinking about, dreaming about."

"No..." It was a soft groan of denial and she shook her head. "I can't believe this is happening!"

"Believe it," Slate murmured. "We both knew this was going to happen from the first moment we set eyes on each other, Jamie. You know that."

"No," she whispered again, almost desperately this time. "I can't let this happen, Slate. It's too dangerous!"

"Dangerous?" He drew back so he could look down at her, seeing something he could have sworn was panic in her eyes. "Jamie, what are you talking about? Is it that man you mentioned? The one you're involved with?"

She stared up at him blankly, not seeming to understand what he was talking about. Then suddenly her eyes widened and she sucked in a horrified breath. "Oh, my God! Curtis! I forgot all about—!"

She caught herself much too late and Slate laughed, pulling her closer. "So you forgot all about him, did you? If he slips your mind during a simple little kiss, Irish..."

"Damn you, stop laughing at me!" But she was laughing herself when she said it, and she didn't resist when he tugged her gently against him. "And that was no 'simple little kiss,' McCall—and you know it!"

"I'd have to try it again just to make sure."

"Not a chance!" She slipped from his embrace and retreated a few steps, managing a breathless laugh. "My mother told me all about men like you, McCall!"

"And what did she tell you?"

"That you're dangerous."

"Do you think I'm dangerous, Jamie?" he asked softly, reaching for her, his fingers closing on moonlight and mist.

"Oh, yes," she whispered unsteadily, her eyes wide and dark. "I think you're the most dangerous kind of all!"

"This," Jamie said disgustedly, "is blatant, unmitigated bribery!"

"Completely shameless," Sam agreed with a laugh. He leaned back against her kitchen counter, shaking his head in amusement. "I'll tell you one thing, Green Eyes—you've done something no one else has ever managed to do: you've got Slate McCall on the ropes. He's ready to do anything to get your help with those bears, including stooping to blatant, unmitigated bribery."

"And how come you never told me until now that you've been working for that man for nearly a month?"

"With, Green Eyes. I'm working *with* McCall, not for."

"Nobody works *with* Slate McCall," Jamie advised him. "He's the original lone wolf. Absolute ruler of his kingdom."

Sam chuckled. "He may be a little light on patience and tact, but he's dead fair. Remember Cornelius? He'd tell you one thing today and the opposite tomorrow, and if it looked like trouble he'd deny telling you anything at all. McCall isn't into power games or corporate politics. He's interested in just one thing—getting that dam built. Nothing else is important."

Jamie raised an expressive eyebrow and handed him a steaming mug of tea. "Tell me again what he said."

"I've told you twice now."

"So tell me again. I love the sound of a man groveling."

Sam gave a snort of laughter. "Funny, he said you'd probably feel that way. What is it between you two, anyway?"

"Nothing," Jamie said swiftly, reaching for the other mug of tea. She walked down into the sunken living room and curled up in her father's big armchair beside the fire.

Sam dropped into the other chair with a contented sigh. "So?"

Sam sighed good-naturedly. "He said that if you help him get rid of the bears with the least amount of damage to both us *and* them, he'll let you back on-site."

"Don't you find his logic a little flawed? Common sense says I'd want to keep the bears at the dump as long as possible."

"I mentioned that to him," Sam admitted with a cheerful grin. "But he figures you'll help him for the same reason I do—because you know better than anyone that when bears and men collide, the bears *always* come out losers." Jamie frowned, swirling her tea pensively. "What's the problem, Jamie? I've never seen you like this before. You're off in some other world half the time, and whenever McCall's name comes up you nearly bite my head off."

"Don't be silly!"

"Hey." Sam speared her with a shrewd gaze. "Come on, Green Eyes. We've been best buddies for over seventeen years now. Hell, we're blood brothers—and we've both got the scars to prove it." Grinning, he held up his right thumb. "Remember when we made that oath to always trust each other, no matter what?"

Smiling in spite of herself, Jamie rubbed her own thumb. The scar there was still visible, and she remembered the solemnity with which they'd made that oath, making the ritual cuts with her father's big hunting knife and holding their thumbs together so their blood mingled. "We were kids then, Sam. Besides, you broke the oath years ago when you married that Mohawk schoolteacher instead of me."

Laughing, Sam reached across with his foot to nudge hers on the hassock they shared. "You ran out on me first to go to college, remember?"

She smiled wistfully. "Things were great back then, weren't they, Sam? Remember how Dad used to take the two of us camping up on the Mountain? And fishing? I can still tie a trout fly that'll bring in a five pounder at every cast."

"I miss him," Sam said quietly.

Jamie nodded, staring down at the mug cupped between her palms, filled with an aching emptiness. "Everything's changing, Sam. Everything I used to know and love is disappearing."

"Hey." Sam set his mug down and leaned forward to capture her hands in his. "I'll always be here, Green Eyes. And Pine Lake. The Mountain."

"Part of the Mountain," Jamie corrected bitterly. "That damned river's taking most of it."

"And giving a lot back," Sam said gently. "Jamie, things can never be the way they were when we were kids. You know that. You've watched the changes—the mine's closed down, the mills will be next. There's no work up here, nothing to keep people from leaving. But the lake that McCall is creating with that dam is giving this whole valley a shot in the arm."

"Oh, I know, I know," Jamie said wearily. "There'll be parks and campgrounds, boat ramps, hiking trails."

"And when the fish hatchery is finished the whole country will be up here after our trout. That big resort they're building will provide jobs for dozens of people before *and* after it's finished. So will all the other motels and restaurants that'll follow. It'll put life back in the Skookum, Jamie. Your dad knew that. That's why he supported the dam even in the beginning when everyone else in the community was dead set against it."

"But it's not going to be *our* valley anymore. Don't you see that, Sam? It's going to belong to—to strangers!"

"Is that why you're thinking of selling the Mountain?"

"I'm not thinking about selling the Mountain," Jamie retorted sharply. "It's simply an option. Something that has to be considered now Dad's gone."

"How much does Curtis think it'll bring?"

Jamie felt herself flush, annoyed at how Sam could still sense her vulnerabilities and hit them with deadly aim.

Sam's black eyes glittered in the firelight. "It's time you made a choice, lady—between the Skookum and the Outside. Between your head and your heart. I know your mother's been playing mind games with you about selling this mountain and getting out for good—hell, she's been playing mind games with you ever since she and your dad broke up. But—''

"They didn't break up," Jamie said defensively.

"Agreed to separate, then. All I know is that for seventeen years you've been torn between them. When your dad was alive you spent half your life defending him to your mother—defending his work, his dreams, even those weeks on end when his only friend was a bottle. And the rest of the year you'd be defending your mother to him. Don't you think I didn't see the hope in your eyes every time he decided to make another go of it in the city and move back in with your mom? Two months later he'd be back here, holed up with a whiskey bottle for as long as it took him to get over disappointing his little girl again. God, Jamie, I ached for you. I knew you wanted to stay up here with him but were afraid of hurting your mother, terrified to be seen taking sides. But Jamie, it's over. You're an adult now—you have to live your life for you, not for her.''

Jamie stared at the mug in her hands, anger flirting through her. And under the anger, that familiar sick, panicky feeling she got whenever she thought of her parents and the impossible conflict of trying to love them both equally, to be a perfect daughter to both, terrified that in their war with each other she'd somehow be forgotten. She took a deep breath, forcing the feeling away. "And you think that's what I'm doing?''

"I know that's what you're doing. Your mother wants nothing more in this world than to see you married to Curtis Winthrop—pardon me, *Doctor* Curtis Winthrop—and become one of those faculty wives *she* always wanted to be.''

"Oh, Sam, quit being so dramatic!'' In spite of herself, Jamie had to laugh. She'd known Sam for too many years to resent his honesty. Even when he was wrong. "What is it you have against Curtis, anyway?''

"The man's using you," he said grimly. "I've seen his type too often while I've been working with the Native Action Committee not to recognize it when I see it. He's just out for himself, Jamie."

"Sam, I know you don't approve of what we're doing up here, but it was Dad who gave Curtis the idea."

"No, it was Curtis who *got* the idea from your dad—there's a difference. Now your dad's dead, Winthrop wants to use his work as a way to get his own name in every scientific journal in the world. And he's convinced you to go along with it. Your dad would never approve of what you guys are doing—and you know it."

"Dad designed the traps in the first place!"

"Sure he did, but purely as a scientific exercise. He sure had no intention of actually *catching* anything!"

"Sam..." Jamie caught her impatience, swallowed it. "Curtis and I are going to be married, so—"

"Damn it, Jamie, how can you just throw your life away like that! What you want is someone like Slate McCall, a real man who loves these mountains as much as you do, who—"

Jamie nearly choked on her tea. "Are you out of your mind?"

"Looks like a match made in heaven from where I stand."

"Well, you definitely need a new perspective!"

"And *you* need a—"

"Sam, I'm warning you."

"Okay, okay." He held both hands up in surrender. "Just tell me your answer to McCall's offer and I won't mention his name again. Except to say that he seems to be suffering from the same affliction you are these days—either staring out the window with a faraway look on his face, or chewing someone out."

"Tell him I'll work up a battle plan—with its advantages and drawbacks spelled out—and send it over to him. He can implement it or not, as he chooses. But *remind* him," she added darkly, "that I expect to see security passes at the main gate for both Terry and me by Monday morning."

"If you're coming in Monday, why not just deliver it to McCall yourself? He'll probably have a thousand questions."

"I'll send it," she repeated in a tone that brooked no argument.

It had been a week since she'd seen Slate. Seven very long, very arduous days. They'd been long and arduous for the simple reason that she wasn't sleeping. And the reason she wasn't sleeping was that every time she closed her eyes she was back in Slate McCall's arms again.

For one rash instant she was tempted to blurt the whole story out to Sam, then she subsided. He'd already admitted his bias. And he never had understood her preference for stable, stolid and totally unadventurous men. All through college he'd given her a bad time about what he called her "oatmeal porridge" dates. "They're all thick, pasty and boring," he'd tell her disgustedly. "Every guy on campus would give his right arm to go out with you, Jamie—and you chose *porridge*!"

Well, maybe they were porridge, but they were safe. You didn't lose your heart to porridge, and you didn't get so swept away by passion with porridge that you forgot what was important in your life. So she'd stuck close to her books and made certain that her male acquaintances were well within the parameters of what her mother called "safe." The "dangerous" men she admired, sometimes a trifle wistfully, from a distance, knowing they were not for her.

Heaven knows, Curtis Winthrop was certainly "safe."

A little twinge of guilt followed the traitorous thought. But there was no denying she sometimes wished their relationship had more excitement. She thought of the rough, earthy passion in Slate's kiss, the unapologetic hunger in his eyes when he'd gazed down at her. His desires were as blunt and uncomplicated as the man himself, and for those few minutes he'd made her feel like the most desirable woman in the world. Hating herself for it, she found herself comparing that kiss to one of Curtis's dry little pecks on the cheek, placed there almost absently when he remembered.

Oh, he made half-hearted attempts at passion now and again, but his embraces were stiff and awkward and his antiseptic kisses always made her feel as though he'd really rather be home reading a book.

And Slate? Oh, Lord—Slate kissed her as though he'd been condemned to death and she was his last meal.

Even thinking about it made her a little breathless and she shoved the vivid images away and sipped her tea, aware that Sam was watching her with an odd little smile.

There was no doubt about it, Slate told himself with some irritation: he was a damned fool. Only fools and fourteen-year-olds—who could be forgiven their irrational behavior on the basis of raging hormones—would go slogging through the swamps and untamed forests of B.C. to find a woman.

Swearing, he batted at the cloud of mosquitoes hovering around his head. His boots squelched with every step and he felt swamp water ooze between his toes. He'd gone right up to his knees that last time, water and muck the color of ink sucking at him. Where in the hell *was* she?

He'd taken a wrong turn, that was the only explanation. He was going to spend the rest of his life wandering this damned fog-shrouded mountain looking for a woman who wasn't even out here. She'd probably gone home when it had started to rain. She was probably curled up in front of a snapping log fire right now, drinking hot buttered rum. Maybe Curtis was there with her. Maybe they were entwined under a warm eiderdown right now, naked, exhausted from an afternoon of erotic excesses. Maybe...

He caught the next maybe before it was even fully formed and shoved it ruthlessly from his mind. The only maybe he should be worrying about was maybe dying out here, soaked to the skin and chewed to pieces by mosquitoes the size of sparrows. A trickle of icy rainwater drooled down the back of his neck and he swore again, louder this time and with considerable feeling.

And then, with absolutely no warning at all, he found her.

All he could see was her head, green eyes wide with surprise as he stepped up onto the jagged outcrop of rock overlooking the spring bubbling up from a cleft in the mountain.

"You have a unique way with words, McCall. I've never heard those last two expressions used together like that before."

"What the hell are you doing?" He stared down at her, realizing that the parts of her he couldn't see were submerged in milky-blue water. "It's barely above freezing!"

"Just," she said cheerfully, lifting her wet arms above her head and stretching languorously. "It was snowing a few minutes ago." She lay her head back against a cushion of moss and closed her eyes, smiling drowsily. "Hot mineral spring, McCall. Heaven on earth on a day like this." One emerald eye opened and took in his muddy boots and jeans, the smears of sweat and dirt on his face, closed again. "You could use a bath yourself. Why didn't you go around that bog instead of through it?"

"I couldn't *find* the around," he growled. He looked down at her, feeling cold rainwater trickle between his shoulder blades, the sting of mosquito welts. "Oh, hell, why not?"

He'd discarded his jacket and was unbuttoning his shirt when her eyes flicked open. She watched in undisguised alarm as he undid the remaining buttons and tugged his shirt out of his jeans. "I didn't necessarily mean right now," she said quickly.

"No reason to wait." He grinned down at her as he folded his shirt and tucked it inside his leather jacket to protect it from the drizzling rain. Perching on the edge of the outcrop, he unlaced his mud-caked boots and pulled them off, then peeled off his sopping socks.

"McCall..." Her eyes widened even more as his hand went to the snap on his jeans. "This pool isn't big enough for—"

"It'll be cozy, but that's fine," he assured her as he unzipped his jeans. "Just pretend we're in the hot tub at a snazzy Tahoe resort. You don't have a bottle of champagne with you, do you?'' He started peeling out of his wet jeans. "Champagne would really hit the spot.''

Seven

The steam rising off the opalescent water made Slate more cautious than he needed to be, and as he lowered himself gingerly into the pool he was relieved to discover it was no hotter than an average bath. The rocks on the sides and bottom of the pool were smooth and slippery and he sank against them with a sigh, wriggling around until he was comfortable, legs stretched out, neck cradled by a loop of pine root upholstered with moss.

The pool was like something out of a fairy tale, wreathed in tendrils of steam and mist, the overhanging grass and wildflowers dripping with rainwater. An ancient, gnarled pine hung out over the water, garlands of mist weaving through its twisted branches.

He could already feel the heat drawing the tension from his muscles and he smiled sleepily. "I've been trying to talk to you all week, Irish." She was watching him warily, near enough to touch had he made the effort. "You've been avoiding me."

"Don't be silly," she replied much too quickly. "Why would I do that?"

"Beats me." He closed his eyes, still smiling. "If I didn't know better, I'd say I'd scared you off." The silence stretched on for so long he didn't think she was going to answer. Then she said, "No..." so unconvincingly he had to swallow a laugh. "That report you sent over was a great piece of work. I've contacted the Alaska parks people about getting one of those bearproof garbage enclosures you mentioned. And I've decided you're right about flying the garbage off the site. It's a hell of an expense, but so's losing a man or two. Or a bear, for that matter."

"You don't waste any time, do you?"

"Nope." He smiled. "And in line with your recommendation, we'll make the transition slowly enough to give your bears time to get used to a depleting food supply. We'll also only approach the dump late at night."

"You're still going to have bears underfoot," she reminded him. "But fewer, and with luck most will be the younger, more easily intimidated ones that get chased away by the hierarchal bears during the day."

"You know," he said with a dry laugh, "this job is teaching me a hell of a lot more about bears than I ever wanted to know."

Jamie's eyes met his, filled with amusement. "In the old days, most Indian cultures believed that a bear was the reincarnated spirit of a brave warrior. And bear-claw necklaces are still highly valued. They're supposed to imbue the wearer with the strength and courage of the animal."

Slate reached out and ran his fingers under the leather thong around her neck, drawing it out of the water until the bear-claw pendant rested in his palm. "Is that what this does?"

She laughed. "Sam Two Elks's grandfather gave it to me when I was ten years old. He told me it was strong medicine—that it would always protect me when I traveled among bears. I think he meant two footed as well as four."

"Does it work?"

"I'm still in one piece."

As hard as he tried, Slate couldn't keep the grin off his mouth. "So I've noticed," he murmured as he let the wet claw slip off his palm. *And a singularly attractive one at that.*

She'd pinned her hair up in a loose knot that had spilled copper tendrils around her neck and face. It was beaded with mist and raindrops that glittered when she moved, and it occurred to Slate that there were women who paid a king's ransom for tiaras and ropes of diamonds to create a less spectacular effect. He could make out the curve of her bare shoulders through the milky water, the indistinct outline of a breast. It started him wondering about what she was wearing, which started him wondering about a number of other things, and a moment or two later he wasn't surprised to discover he'd broken into a sweat.

"So what does Curtis think of all this bear business?"

"Curtis?" She gave him a perplexed look. Then her eyes suddenly narrowed, bright with suspicion. "Has Sam been talking to you?"

Slate shook his head, mystified by her reaction. Jamie settled back against the rocks again, her expression still wary. He made a mental note to talk to Sam just as soon as he got back to camp. "So, tell me," he persevered. "What's this Curtis guy do for a living?"

"He's an anthropologist," she replied a bit stiffly. "Dr. Curtis Winthrop. I'm sure you've heard of him."

"Can't say as I have. But then, I don't spend a lot of time hobnobbing with doctors of any kind."

Jamie gave him a sharp look, knowing damned well he was laughing at her. "Well, he probably hasn't heard of you, either." Which was undoubtedly just as well, she reminded herself. What in heaven's name would Curtis think if he could see her now? "His father is Dr. Gilbert Winthrop. I'm sure you've heard of *him*."

"Africa," Slate said, grinning like the class troublemaker who's just outsmarted his teacher. "Dr. Leaky. The missing link."

"Very *good*, Mr. McCall," Jamie said in her best schoolteacher's voice. "He's one of today's foremost anthropologists. You must have heard his name in Brazil. He's credited with the discovery, on a tributary of the Amazon, of a tribe of Indians that were thought to have vanished centuries ago."

"Quite an act for poor Curtis to follow," Slate drawled.

"Damn that Sam! He *has* been talking to you!"

Slate's pale golden eyes were amused. "Honey, I swear to you that Sam hasn't said a word to me about you *or* Curtis."

She gave him a sharp, mistrustful look, finding it difficult to believe he could have zeroed in on Curtis's frustration with always having his own successes measured against his father's without a little help from Sam. "Curtis," she said forcefully, "is a highly respected scientist in his own right."

Slate was looking at her speculatively and Jamie realized she'd been a little too defensive. Damn him, he was as cunning as one of her own bears, quick to spot the slightest vulnerability.

"And is he in on this little monster hunt you're conducting up here? I was wondering how an underpaid biologist living off college grants managed to finance a sophisticated, state-of-the-art setup like that."

Jamie had her mouth open to tell him to mind his own business when she realized it was pointless. He'd simply push and push until he got the answers he wanted anyway, and Curtis's involvement was hardly a state secret. "Curtis is on the faculty of the University of Washington, and he pulled a few strings to get me a grant. Actually I have enough credibility that I probably could have gotten it without Curtis's help, but it was his idea to get grant money from the anthropology department and use *it* to build the traps and put the monitoring system together. It's on the books as a zoology grant, of course." She smiled humorlessly. "Chasing monsters still isn't considered valid in most scientific circles. Prying grant money loose for what in their terms is legitimate research is tough enough; asking for money to finance a scheme to trap a Sasquatch would get you laughed off campus.''

"Even with the esteemed Dr. Gilbert Winthrop behind you?''

"Dr. Winthrop thinks Curtis's interest in cryptozoology is a waste of—''

"Crypto—*what*? God Almighty, I just think I've got all you *ologists* straight, and you hit me with another one!''

Jamie laughed at the expression on Slate's face. "It's the study of previously unknown species—like the plankton-eating shark discovered off Hawaii in 1976—or animals that have been rediscovered that were thought to be extinct, like the black-footed ferret.''

"And that's not Winthrop Senior's cup of tea.''

"It's not that aspect of it that Dr. Winthrop objects to, it's the fact that many scientists think cryptozoologists are crackpots because they openly admit they're after bigger game: things like the Loch Ness monster, yeti, bigfoot, Mokele-Mbêmbe—that's an amphibious dinosaur report-edly seen in Central Africa.''

"Are they? Crackpots, I mean?''

"I don't think my father was a crackpot, if that's what you mean.''

"That's not what I asked you.''

"I...oh, hell, I don't know!'' Jamie shook her head in weary resignation. "I'm a bear biologist—''

"Interesting imagery there, Ms. Kilpatrick.''

"—who doesn't pretend to know all the answers,'' Jamie went on, ignoring him. "But I do know there are a lot of things in this world that aren't easily explained. I'd hate to think we knew everything there is to know about life on this planet.''

"And whoever does find one of these mystery beasties will sure as hell go down in history. Is that why Curtis is trying his hand at it? I doubt there are many breakthrough discoveries left in the field of anthropology for him to make his name on.''

NO COST! NO OBLIGATION TO BUY!
NO PURCHASE NECESSARY!

PLAY "LUCKY 7"
AND GET AS MANY AS SIX FREE GIFTS . . .

HOW TO PLAY:

1. With a coin, carefully scratch off the silver box at the right. This makes you eligible to receive one or more free books, and possibly other gifts, depending on what is revealed beneath the scratch-off area.

2. You'll receive brand-new Silhouette Desire® novels. When you return this card, we'll send you the books and gifts you qualify for *absolutely free*!

3. Unless you tell us otherwise, every month we'll send you 6 additional novels to read and enjoy. If you decide to keep them, you'll pay only $2.24* per book—that's 26¢ less per book than the cover price plus only 69¢ postage and handling for the entire shipment!

4. When you subscribe to Silhouette Books, we'll also send you additional free gifts from time to time as a token of our appreciation for being a home subscriber.

5. You must be completely satisfied. You may cancel at any time simply by writing "cancel" on your statement or returning a shipment of books to us at our cost.

*Terms and prices subject to change without notice.

You'll love your elegant bracelet watch—
this classic LCD Quartz Watch is a perfect
expression of your style and good taste—
and it is yours FREE as an added thanks for
giving our Reader Service a try.

PLAY "LUCKY 7"

Just scratch off the silver box with a coin.
Then check below to see which gifts you get.

YES! I have scratched off the silver box. Please send me all the
gifts for which I qualify. I understand I am under no obligation
to purchase any books, as explained on the opposite page.

326 CIS 814B

NAME

ADDRESS   APT

CITY   PROVINCE   POSTAL CODE

7	7	7	WORTH FOUR FREE BOOKS. FREE BRACELET WATCH AND MYSTERY BONUS
🍒	🍒	🍒	WORTH FOUR FREE BOOKS AND MYSTERY BONUS
●	●	●	WORTH FOUR FREE BOOKS
🔔	🔔	🍒	WORTH TWO FREE BOOKS

Canada Post
Postes Canada
125

DETACH AND MAIL CARD TODAY

It was uncanny how he homed in on things. It must have something to do with the way an engineer's mind worked—the ability to see a completed picture from a rough sketch. She thought of the frustrated anger on Curtis's face whenever his father's name came up, how he'd once said, "There's nothing left to discover! He's done it all—he hasn't left a damned thing for me but crumbs."

"How come he isn't up here with you?"

Jamie looked at him in annoyance. "Why are you so fascinated with Curtis Winthrop, anyway?"

"I'm not," Slate said with his usual bluntness. "I just want to know how fascinated *you* are."

"And what makes that your business?"

"A hell of a lot, considering I want to sleep with his woman."

It wasn't quite how he'd intended to put it, but once the words were said there didn't seem to be any point in retracting them. The dumbfounded expression on Jamie's face made him chuckle. "Well, there's a little more to it than that, I guess, but you get my drift."

"I...I..." She seemed to be having trouble catching her breath. "I think I do," she finally got out in a rather squeaky whisper. "Are you always this...honest?"

Slate met her wide-eyed stare evenly. "Does it bother you?"

"I..." She closed her eyes, took a long, deep breath, opened them. "I've never had anybody just come out and say it like that."

"I don't play games, Jamie."

"No. I can see that." She still looked a little shaken, but she'd gotten some of her color back. "I can't believe I'm taking this so calmly." She gave an unsteady laugh. "I mean, I'm sitting half-naked beside a man I hardly know who has just told me he wants to take me to bed, and I haven't screamed or anything."

"You know me," Slate said softly, reaching for her. "You know everything about me, Jamie Kilpatrick...."

"No—no...." But it was no more than an unsteady whisper and Jamie heard the want in her voice, saw the answering want in his eyes as his large, warm hands clasped her by the waist and pulled her gently toward him. "Oh, no, Slate," she whispered pleadingly. "Please don't do this to me!"

Yet she wanted it to happen. Wanted to feel his muscular arms around her again, wanted his mouth on hers again doing all those wondrous, magical things that had sent her senses whirling and her willpower spinning away like a leaf on the wind.

He drew her in close to him and their drifting legs intertwined, and Jamie shook her head numbly. "No," she whispered, bracing her outstretched palms against his chest. "No, I can't do this. It's too dangerous."

"You know it's what you want," Slate murmured, one hand gliding up her back while the other cupped her hip, supporting her against the buoyancy of the water.

There's still time. Desperately she kept repeating it to herself, a talisman against the temptation drawing her ever deeper into danger. There's still time. Time to escape.... Her splayed fingers skated across his wet chest and she felt the ripple of muscle as he breathed, the deep rhythmic beat of his heart. The rain had turned to snow and she watched the flakes settle on his hair and shoulders, melt even as she was melting.

"Tell me, Jamie," he coaxed in a caramel purr. "Tell me to stop, and I'll stop. Tell me you don't want me, and I'll leave right now."

It was there—the escape she wanted. One simple, two-letter word was all it would take. He'd release her from his spell and she'd never again have to lie awake at night, half-mad with the wanting, never again spend her days in dread and anticipation waiting for the wolf-eyed man, the dangerous man, to step silently from the forest and steal her heart.

"Say it, Jamie," he was whispering, the warmth of his breath on her mouth, her throat, the hollow under her ear. "Say you don't want me."

...*still time*... Her hands glided almost of their own accord to his shoulders and she felt herself drift into the circle of his arms, the touch of his mouth on her throat making her go shivery inside. Snowflakes clung to his neck and she felt them melt on her tongue as she licked them away. She rubbed her cheek against the male roughness of his and heard his breath catch. He cupped her face and turned it so her lips were under his.

His mouth was hot and urgent and he kissed her with none of the gentleness of that first time. There was no slow teasing, no coaxing, just hot hungry want, his tongue thrusting in and possessing hers without preamble or hesitation. His kiss was exactly as she'd known it would be, deep and hard and aggressive, as brash and unapologetically physical as the man himself. He knew exactly what he wanted and he took it, knew just as certainly what she needed and gave it. He needed no reasons, no philosophizing about the rightness or wrongness of it, and Jamie, with one last, despairing apology to Curtis and her mother, simply relaxed in his arms and kissed him back with all the passion she could no longer deny.

Intoxicated with the taste of her, the feel of her all warm and slippery in his hands, Slate felt reality slide and spiral away. It was like getting caught in the outflow of a dam, spun down and around until everything melted away in a dizzying blur and all hope of safety vanished.

There was no escape. Not this time. This time he was caught and there wouldn't be any fighting free.

And this time, he realized with faint wonder, he didn't even want freedom.

He ran his hands up and down her back, marveling how anything so lithe and smoothly muscled could be so meltingly soft. He caught her thigh between his and pressed himself against her, hearing her breath catch and then his own in concert as she arched her back and pressed against him. Her hands were traveling now, settling on his hips. He moved his pelvis against her and she moaned softly, her head falling back to bare her throat to his mouth. Her hair spilled free of the pins and cascaded into the water and Slate felt it swirl around them, silken fire in the milk-blue water.

The narrow band of her bra was under his hand and, hardly aware of what he was doing, he unclasped it. It floated to the surface and her bared breasts brushed his chest, filled his hands. Jamie moaned softly and suddenly her breasts were clear of the water and Slate filled his mouth greedily. Her hands flexed on his shoulders and she whispered his name in a breathless voice, cradled his head in her arms. Slowly her wet body slid through his hands and his mouth trailed from breast to throat, to the curl of her ear, down again to her mouth.

"Oh, Slate," she moaned. "I shouldn't be letting this happen."

"This is exactly what's supposed to be happening," Slate murmured against her mouth. "It's right, Jamie. It's right for both of us."

"But I'm scared...."

"Of me?"

"Of me!" She fit her mouth perfectly to his and he kissed her deeply, felt her tremble, felt the bright splintering fires of his own need take flame. "I'm scared to let go," she sobbed against his mouth. "Scared of what's going to happen if I do."

"Do you trust me?"

She murmured something against his mouth and he kissed her, felt his willpower go nearly tumbling away as she fit herself with precision against him. He moved his pelvis gently and she moaned deep in her throat, a shudder running through her as she moved her hips in rhythmic counterpoint to his, her mouth softening, melting under his.

"Is that yes?" He groaned against her lips. "Jamie, another minute and it's going to be way too late. We can stop but you've got to tell me now!"

She drew back very slightly, her eyes wide as they looked into his. "I don't want to stop," she whispered. "I know I should, but—"

Slate pulled her close against him, lowering his mouth to hers, and she gave a sigh of satisfaction and kissed him with a rough, urgent passion that left them both panting. "Show me," she moaned. "Show me what it's like, Slate. I want you . . . I want you so badly. I *need* you . . . ."

She moved against him again and Slate groaned, knowing he was lost. From the moment she'd caught him in that forest trap he'd lost his will to be free. Desire, infatuation, love . . . he had no idea of its name, only that it held him in chains far stronger than steel. And that all the paths of his life had led to this place and this moment.

He eased her gently out of the wisp of fabric around her hips and slowly, gently, showed her how to love. He was at first surprised, then touched, to discover how inexperienced she was, awkward and shy at one moment yet deliciously uninhibited the next. He taught her things about her own body she'd never known before, and things about his she'd never dreamed. And finally, when neither of them could wait any longer, he eased her into his lap and down over his own flesh, losing himself in the willing heat of her body.

It was snowing harder now, and the steam from the hot pool swirled around Jamie as she sat fully astride him, her wet body gleaming like silk. Eyes closed, she moved sinuously on him, around him. Her head fell back and her hair spilled like liquid fire to the water behind her, snowflakes caught in its copper tangles like jewels. She was as taut as a bow and Slate ran his hands slowly up her ribs to her breasts and caressed them.

She was like silken fire around him, each long honeyed thrust of her hips bringing him nearer and nearer the edge. Yet he held himself back, luxuriating in watching her explore and savor every new sensation, every moment of growing pleasure. Slowly he could sense the tension within her grow. The rhythmic swing of her hips faltered, became uneven as she sought to capture the elusive release that was so close yet so tantalizingly out of reach. She caught her lower lip between her teeth and he knew by the change in her breathing that she was close, so close... yet still too unfamiliar with her own body and needs to take herself that final distance.

Gently he ran his hands from her hips to her thighs, then lower still. His fingers found her, caressed her, and she gave a long, soft cry of wonder. He felt the tremors within her, felt her go absolutely motionless for a heartbeat of time. Then it broke and spilled through her and she gave another soft cry, this one of pure pleasure.

His own release came moments later, enjoyed all the more for knowing he'd made it as close to perfect for her as he could, and as they lay in each other's arms, Slate knew that nothing could come even close to the contentment he felt.

She had to be dreaming.

Jamie kept her eyes firmly closed and let her mind simply drift. She dreamed she was lying in Slate's arms, his lean body locked intimately with hers, his hand cupping her head against his shoulder. They were in the hot mineral spring up on Skookum Mountain, wreathed in mist and steam while it gently snowed around them, and they had just made love. The dream had been deliciously explicit this time, every detail of their love play so real she could still feel the tiny aftertremors of that last incredible moment. Before, she'd always wakened too soon and had been forced to spend the rest of the night in restless, unfulfilled torment. But this time...

This time it was real.

Impossible, but real. For twenty-eight years she'd been listening to her mother's warnings about dangerous men. For the last twelve of those she'd resisted even the most ardent pursuers. And for what? Fourteen days after pulling this hardheaded, incredibly annoying man out of the ground, she was lying naked with him in a hot spring, still flushed from their tempestuous lovemaking.

"Oh, God." She closed her eyes. It was terrifying how easily he'd recognized the passion lying dormant in her, had coaxed ember to flame and had set her afire as she'd never burned before. For those long, delicious minutes in his arms she hadn't cared about her work or Curtis or even her bears. Nothing in the universe had mattered but being with him, being part of him. Exactly as her mother had warned.

"I've got to go." She sat straight up. Water cascaded off her and she crossed her arms over her breasts, suddenly very conscious of her nakedness.

Slate grinned lazily and settled his hands firmly on her hips. "Wait a while, Irish. I promise I'll make it worth your while."

The promising heat in those smiling amber eyes made her blush. "No. I—really, I've got to go. Now." She could hear the panic in her voice, knew by the puzzled expression on his face that he heard it, too. But she didn't care. She had to get away before it was too late. She was powerless against whatever magic he wielded, she knew that now.

But first, she had to get out of this damned pool. Arms still crossed protectively, she realized with a sinking heart that the only way she could ease herself free of Slate was to brace her hands on his shoulders. Which meant not just baring herself to him but leaning over him, as seductive a move as any man could want. And then, with Slate as a rapt observer, she had to clamber out of the pool itself, as naked as the day she was born, collect her clothes and get dressed.

"I...uh..." She swallowed, knowing her cheeks were scarlet. "Would you mind closing your eyes?" Slate gave her a look of such amused disbelief that she blushed even harder. "Please!" Smiling indulgently, Slate nodded and dutifully closed his eyes and Jamie slipped off him swiftly.

"Can I look now?"

Eight

——

The husky purr made Jamie lose her grip on the slippery rocks along the edge of the pool and she floundered for a moment, nearly going over her head. "No! Please, Slate, it's—"

"Hey, Irish, it's okay," he said softly. "When you're ready, let me know."

In that instant, she nearly faltered. Curtis would have told her to stop acting like a child. Actually Curtis wouldn't have said anything because he'd have died before making love outdoors, let alone in a bubbling hot spring on the side of a mountain in a spring snow flurry. She didn't even know if Curtis *made* love. He certainly hadn't with her. She'd convinced herself it didn't matter. That once they were married he'd be different. But now, having discovered just how wondrous it could be with a thoughtful, uninhibited and thoroughly lustful man...

She stopped the thought before it got any further and scrambled out of the pool and into her clothes as though aiming for a Guinness record.

"Jamie!" She was halfway across the rock outcrop and almost into the trees before he called out to her. She nearly broke into a run, intending to sprint into the forest where she could lose him easily, then make her way down to her cabin alone. But she hesitated as he called again, his voice impatient and puzzled. She'd have to face him sooner or later. If he didn't find her tonight, he'd find her tomorrow or the next day. He wasn't the kind of man who could be eluded for long.

She stopped where the rock outcropping ended in a cliff overlooking the valley and waited for him in the shelter of a stand of tall cedars.

He was still buttoning his shirt when he caught up to her. He tucked it into his jeans and pulled on his thick Irish knit pullover without saying anything, then braced his shoulder against a tree and looked down at her. "That was a pretty quick getaway you made back there, Irish." His gaze held hers, his expression guarded. Questioning. "What's going on?"

"Nothing." Jamie shoved her hands into the pockets of her down vest, shoulders hunched against the wind. "I just have to go. I have a lot of work to do, that's all."

Frowning slightly, he reached out and cupped her cheek in his hand and bent down to kiss her. Jamie wrenched away from him, feeling her heart give a treacherous little leap at even so innocent a touch. Slate blew a long breath between his teeth, his eyes narrowed. "What's this all about, Jamie?" he asked calmly.

"This should never have happened." She stared across the valley, at the cold tall peaks. "I didn't intend things to go quite that ... far."

"You weren't seduced, Jamie," he said with a hint of irritation in his voice. "You knew exactly what you were doing."

"I know that!" Somehow, the truth made it worse. "I got swept up and carried away, and now I ... I wish I hadn't. That's all."

"What the hell are you saying?" His voice was dangerously soft. "That this was just a magical afternoon that ends when we leave the mountain?"

"Exactly."

"I don't believe in fairy tales," he said bluntly. "What happened this afternoon *was* magic—or the nearest thing to it I've encountered."

How could she deny that? She dropped her gaze. "I want you to forget it happened at all."

He gave a bark of astonished laughter. "For crying out loud, Jamie! Do you think I do this sort of thing every day? That I'll just wipe out the memory of today with a dozen more like it?"

"I've spent most of my life around construction camps and the men who work in them. Every woman you meet is the passion of your life—until the next one. I was just one afternoon's passion, Slate. Not worth remembering."

"Damn it, Jamie, what the—" He bit it off. Took a deep breath and said evenly, "I just hope Winthrop knows how lucky he is."

"Curtis doesn't have anything to do with this."

"He's got everything to do with this," he growled. "If he was doing his job properly in the first place, this never would have happened."

She kept her eyes on those cold, distant mountains, knowing he was being deliberately crude just to get a reaction from her. "Curtis and I have a . . . different sort of relationship," she said primly. "It's based on respect and . . . and other things. Not lust."

"I could tell," he drawled. "You haven't taken part in any good old-fashioned lust for a long while." Her cheeks flamed, and Slate sighed. "Come on, Irish. What's the real story here?"

"The real story is that you and I had a spur-of-the-moment fling that is never going to be repeated. It was pleasant. Both of us enjoyed it, but—"

"Pleasant?" His voice startled a raven out of a nearby tree. "You call what we had today *pleasant*? What the hell

were you doing—conducting a behavioral study? Mating techniques of the adult male?'' He swore under his breath and wheeled away from her, fingers shoved into the front pockets of his jeans, shoulders stiff under the leather jacket. He stared out across the valley, an angry silhouette against the sky. "If you think you're getting rid of me that easily, you'd better think again."

Jamie's heart gave a thump. "Please, Slate, we—"

"Do you love him?" He asked it with the same unapologetic bluntness with which he did everything in his life, and he turned and gave her a long, searching look. Jamie looked away and he swore softly. "Look at me, Jamie." Unwillingly she lifted her gaze to his. "Say it," he told her. "Tell me you love Curtis Winthrop, and that'll be the end of it. Say it!"

"No, I don't love him!" It was torn from her before she could stop it and she gave a sob of relief and despair, tucking her head down so Slate couldn't see the sudden tears in her eyes. "Are you satisfied now?"

"Then why...?" He put his fingers under her chin and tipped her face up, his expression puzzled and frowning.

"Because I'm scared!" Again, it was out before she could stop it. She tried to laugh, gazing up at Slate miserably. "Curtis is safe. Don't you understand that? When he kisses me I don't feel a thing, and that makes him safe! I'll marry him and be Mrs. Curtis Winthrop and I'll put on faculty teas and live in a nice house in Seattle with—"

"—with a white picket fence and a lawn mower," Slate finished for her. "And you think that's going to make you happy?"

"Happier than you'll make me, Slater McCall," she whispered.

"I doubt that," he growled. "I doubt that a hell of a lot."

"I'll have a secure life with Curtis."

He swore wearily and combed his wet hair back with his fingers. "That's your mother talking, Jamie, not you. She blames your father for all the unhappiness in her life, and wants to protect you by seeing you don't make the same mistake. She'd rather see you throw your life away on a man you don't love than take a risk on real love. Real passion."

"Passion!" Jamie's anger was real now. "Passion is an illusion."

"Passion," Slate said tightly, "is what kept your father searching for Sasquatch in spite of criticism and disbelief. Passion is what brought you into my office demanding to be allowed to continue your study at the dump. And passion," he added with a narrow-eyed look, "is what's going to bring you back into my arms when you finally admit you're not the kind of woman who can settle for safe and secure!" He turned on his heel and strode down the trail, not even looking back.

Scared of him. Slate shook his head. That was something new. He'd had women mad at him before. He'd even had women in love with him before. But he'd never had one so scared of him he could see the panic in her eyes every time she looked at him.

He sighed and shook his head again. Damn it, he wasn't any good at this sort of thing. Women had always been a mystery to him. Delightful and wondrous creatures, but a mystery. He could walk along a valley and know exactly where the dam should go. He could look at a core sample brought up from a riverbed and tell the porosity of the rock down to three decimal places. He could erect a tall, curving wing of concrete that would hold back a river. But there was no way he could figure out what made women tick. They didn't respond to the normal laws of the universe, and the engineering manual had never been written that told him how to decipher them.

If he had any damned sense at all, he'd be relieved that she was calling it off this cleanly. If they had continued, they'd just have gotten all tangled up in each other's lives— she'd fall in love with him or he'd fall in love with her and someone would get hurt. His wasn't the kind of life you built foundations on; it was made up of single moments in time, a patchwork quilt of people and places and memories. In eighteen months the Skookum would be behind him and he'd be on his way to another valley, another river, another dam. She'd done them both a favor, ending it before either had made the mistake of caring.

He was still thinking about this five minutes later when he suddenly realized he was lost.

He stopped and looked around him, frowning. The forest was thick here, utterly silent but for the patter of dripping water on the thick carpet of moss and pine needles. The trees rose around him like ghostly pillars, their tops lost in rain and cloud. It was dim and still and Slate found himself holding his breath, listening.

Now what? He could keep going and hope he hit something he recognized, or go back to the hot spring and start over. He glanced at the sky, but there was nothing above him but a pewter haze that relinquished no clue as to what direction he was facing. It would be dark before long. He took another impatient glance around him, then decided to risk the unknown and continued in the direction he'd been going.

He didn't see the grizzly until he was practically on him. The path had widened into a small misty clearing and he was half across it before a movement in the corner of his eye made him glance around curiously—and feel his blood run cold.

The big bear had flipped over a rotted log and was rummaging through the debris when Slate appeared in front of him. He gave a startled woof and swung his head up, peering at the intruder. Slate felt his blood drumming in his ears and he swallowed, trying to remember everything he'd ever read about grizzlies. They could swim but couldn't climb well...or was it the other way around? It didn't matter. The river, even if he could find it, was three miles away and the only trees were mature firs and cedars, their trunks straight and smooth for thirty or more feet to the first branches.

"Don't move!"

The quiet voice came from right behind him, and Slate's heart nearly stopped on the spot. "Jamie?"

Her hand slipped into his, her fingers icy. "Don't move."

He appreciated the advice, but it was hardly necessary. He couldn't have moved if someone had tossed a hand grenade at him. The bear took a couple of steps toward them, muzzle lifted, his big nose wriggling. His coat was golden brown frosted with silver, the prominent shoulder hump and long, dished muzzle of his species unmistakable, and he looked like something out of Slate's worst nightmare. The bear gave a guttural sound that was half growl, half groan, and swung his big head back and forth in a gesture of defiance and warning.

"Slate," Jamie whispered urgently, "do *exactly* as I tell you. Move backward with me, very slowly. Don't make any sudden moves, and don't look him in the eyes—he'll feel threatened."

He'll feel threatened? he wanted to shout. Instead, he took one very cautious step backward. The grizzly took another step nearer, then rose onto his back feet and peered intently at them. He gave a coughing grunt and tossed his head, and Slate took another step back, fingers tightening involuntarily on Jamie's.

"He's trying to warn us off. That's a good sign," Jamie murmured. "If he can force us to back down, that makes him dominant. Then he can make a safe retreat himself without losing face and he won't need to charge. But if he does, for God's sake don't run! Hit the ground and curl up with your hands locked around the back of your neck. Protect your face and throat with your arms and knees. And don't fight him. No matter what he does, just play dead."

The grizzly gave another of those eerie moans and shook his head, wet mouth open and gleaming with teeth. He stood seven feet tall, easily, and Slate could see the huge curved claws tipping the forepaws, the glint of intelligence in the piggy eyes. And then, with a coughing grunt, the bear dropped to all fours. He stood there for a minute or two, as though undecided, then he gave the dead log a ferocious swipe with his paw that sent it tumbling across the clearing and walked slowly and with great dignity into the trees.

"My God," Jamie whispered, "wasn't he magnificent?"

"That," Slate replied hoarsely, "is not the first word that comes to mind." He closed his eyes for a moment, relieved to discover his heart hadn't stopped permanently, after all. "Where in the *hell* did you come from? Not that I'm complaining."

It seemed to remind her that her hand was still in his. She pulled it free and shoved both hands into her vest pockets, shrugging. "I, uh, followed you. You went charging down that trail like you knew where you were going, but it can be tricky. There's a turn-off about a mile back that takes you down to the logging road where you left your truck. But if you miss it—"

"—like I did."

"Like you did," she repeated with the faintest hint of a smile, "you wind up following Devil's Cache Creek right into Washington. The next sign of civilization is about 120 miles due south—presuming you got through the snow in Cache Pass. Or across the creek where the trail crosses it just above Has-No-Bottom Falls." Her smile widened slightly at his expression. "The Indians claim the surge pool below the falls is bottomless because anything thrown in—like enemy warriors taken in battle—doesn't come up for years. Dad just figured the water currents force debris into an underwater cavern, but no one's gone down to test his theory. Or the Indians', for that matter."

"I think I'll pass, too," Slate assured her. "And thanks. For coming after me, I mean."

She shrugged it off lightly, starting to walk back up the trail. "These mountains can be dangerous if you don't know your way around. It's a hassle for everyone when somebody gets lost."

"Meaning you were just doing your civic duty," he said dryly, falling into step beside her, "not that you were worried about me."

"Exactly."

"Will that old fellow be back? I've heard of grizzlies circling around to take you by surprise."

Jamie shook her head. "He's puttered off on bear business of his own. That swipe he gave the log was for our benefit—just to show us what he could have done to us if he'd felt like it. Bears enjoy intimidation. It amuses them, I think."

"Believe me," he muttered, "it worked! I figured I was a goner. I had no idea what he was going to do next."

Jamie gave a quiet laugh. "There's an old saying—if you know what a bear's going to do next, you know more than the bear does. No two will ever react the same way to a given situation, and nine times out of ten even the *same* bear won't react the same way twice. They're completely unpredictable." She grinned suddenly. "You should be flattered, actually. That was old Lucifer. He's been a legend in this country for about twenty years. I've only seen him once before myself, when I was about twelve, but I've sure heard lots about him!"

Slate smiled, amused by her exuberance. Excitement had brought the color out in her cheeks and her eyes danced. He reached out and ran his fingers under the leather thong around her neck, drew the claw pendant up from the neck of her shirt. It lay in his palm, warm from where it had nestled between her breasts. "I'd say this thing earned its weight in gold today."

"It's never failed me." Her eyes were very wide, very near.

Slate let the pendant slide between his fingers. The back of his hand was still resting against her throat and he drew it away slowly, letting his fingers linger on the warm, smooth skin. His gaze moved caressingly from feature to fine-boned feature, memorizing the pattern of freckles across the bridge of her nose, the fine scar just under her lower lip where she'd probably fallen as a child. Her gaze locked with his. "You know, Jamie Kilpatrick," he said very quietly, "if a man wasn't very careful, he could get himself seriously hooked on you."

"Please," she whispered, her voice broken. "Don't do this to me, Slate. It would never work."

"Never's a long time, Irish." He bent down and brushed her lips with his. "And don't ever say the word 'impossible' to an engineer—unless you're daring him. Every dam I build is 'impossible.' And I haven't failed yet."

"Slate."

"Come on." He wrapped his fingers around hers. "Let's get out of here before old Lucifer changes his mind about lunch."

Nine

Four days.

It seemed like forever.

It had been four days since he'd seen Jamie, four days since that incredible afternoon at the pool. Four days of hell, each day haunted from dawn to dusk by a woman he couldn't have.

The wind moaned in the crags of the cliff face below him and Slate shrugged his shoulders a little deeper into his jacket. This was one of his favorite viewpoints, high on the mountainside overlooking the river. It gave him an unobstructed view of the entire construction site and the valley to either side. And his dam.

He stared down at it, forcing his mind from its troubled brooding.

In the moonlight, the dam looked like white marble. It could have been an ancient Greek temple standing between two dark shoulders of mountain, put there by some forgotten king. Rising in serene splendor above the mud and rubble, it glowed with an unearthly beauty in the harsh glare of the construction flood lamps. Garlands of lights criss-crossed the gorge above and around it, turning night into day. Even the cranes were strung with work lamps and Slate watched the long booms swing back and forth, clearly outlined against the black sky.

His dam. In spite of his gloom, Slate managed a faint smile. It was crazy, feeling so proprietary about a structure of concrete and steel and iron that until a month ago had been another man's dream. But right from the instant he'd accepted this job, she'd become *his* dam, *his* dream.

He let his gaze drift slowly over the floodlit scene below him, some instinct he was only half-aware of telling him that everything was as it should be. On the upstream side, held at bay by the curving barrier of the coffer dam, the lake that would eventually fill the valley was already starting to rise.

Involuntarily he glanced north to where the looming bulk of Skookum Mountain brooded against the starlit sky. Jamie's mountain. As unyielding and regal as the lady herself.

He swore at himself and turned his gaze stubbornly back to the dam. "She made it plain enough she didn't want anything to do with you," he growled under his breath. "Why don't you get that through your thick skull, McCall?"

Maybe it was because *he* was used to calling the shots, he brooded. In the past, he'd been the one to break off relationships when things seemed to be getting too serious. He'd always told himself it was better that way, that letting a woman fall in love with him when he'd be out of her life a few months down the road was cruel.

Or maybe he'd just been running away. Maybe he'd been using those dams to barricade his heart as solidly as they barricaded the rivers they spanned. Dams might kill you, but they didn't break your heart. They didn't make demands a man couldn't fulfill.

But they couldn't love you back, either. Fleshed in concrete and steel, they couldn't share your dreams, couldn't ease your fears, couldn't fill that empty spot in a man's heart with love and laughter. But a woman could. A woman like Jamie Kilpatrick could.

He swore again. He was too old for all this cosmic soul-searching. He was a dam builder, not a philosopher. Forget about her, he told himself angrily. Taking on the Skookum's enough of a challenge for any man; taking on Jamie Kilpatrick is pure madness.

He was just going to turn away and walk back to his trailer when a flicker of movement on the other side of the river caught his eye. Something was in the trees just beyond the security fence, watching the site. It moved again, just shadow on shadow, and Slate frowned. It was big, whatever it was. And stealthy. It was staying in the shadows under the trees, obviously not wanting to be seen while it watched the construction going on below. And then, suddenly, it stepped into the moonlight.

"What the hell...?" Slate peered across at it, wishing he'd brought his binoculars. It was huge and furred and massively muscled, and in the next instant it had reared onto its hind legs as though to get a better look at the site. It stood there for a long, unmoving moment, gazing curiously at the savage destruction around it, then it shuffled into the darkness under the trees again and disappeared.

Slate didn't even realize he'd been holding his breath until he let it out in a loud *huff*. Lucifer! The old grizzly must have been attracted by the activity and had decided to come by and see what was going on. Curious, or looking for an easy meal?

He could turn into a problem. Slate swore under his breath and turned to walk up to his trailer. As though he didn't have his hands full enough with Jamie's thirty or so black bears, now he had a mountain legend to worry about.

He suddenly stopped, frowning. Lucifer was a deep golden brown, wasn't he? Whatever he'd seen tonight had looked almost silver. Did that mean there was *another* grizzly out there, or was the light just playing tricks on his eyes? For that matter, how did he know it *was* a bear? All he'd seen was a large, furry shape. And yet, what else would it have been—unless he'd just seen his first Sasquatch.

He grinned. This whole valley was starting to do a number on him, no doubt about it. First he'd managed to convince himself he was halfway in love with Jamie Kilpatrick; now he was seeing large hairy apes and talking to himself!

"Yo! McCall!"

Slate glanced up, squinting into the sun. Sam Two Elks grinned down at him, hard hat tilted at a cocky angle. "You got a minute?"

Down on one knee poring over an electrical blueprint, Slate lifted his hand in acknowledgment. He finished giving his instructions to the two electricians hunkered beside him, then stood up, wincing at a twinge in his left knee.

"That knee still bothering you?" Sam asked.

"It stiffens some when the weather acts up, that's all."

"I'm telling you, McCall, my grandmother can fix it for you in no time. She'll whip up a compress of grasses and barks boiled in porcupine fat, and you'll be kicking butt in no time at all."

"I won't have any trouble kicking yours if you don't get off my case," Slate grumbled. "Does your grandmother have a license to practice medicine?"

"She's been doctoring everyone in this valley for sixty years. Hell, she midwived most of the people in this valley!" He fell into step beside Slate and they started walking back toward the untidy collection of construction trailers that acted as engineering and staff site offices. "Some official type from the provincial-government offices called me last night. Seems we're going to get our rec center and hockey arena."

"And you doubted me," Slate said with a laugh. "Mayor's office over in Pine Lake called to say they've got provincial approval to start taking tenders for three ski runs, a chair lift and chalet up on Razorback."

"A lot of people in this valley owe you their thanks," Sam said quietly. "This dam saved the Skookum, no doubt about it."

"And the rest of them figure we've ruined everything," Slate reminded him dryly. "The truth's probably somewhere in between. I just hope the powers that be don't let the developers run wild—it'd be a shame to see this valley turned into an amusement park. I like to think that the great-grandchildren of Jamie's bears will be rambling around these mountains long after we're gone."

"If Jamie has anything to say about it, they will." Sam grinned slyly. "Speaking of which, I hear that boyfriend of hers will be up here this weekend."

Slate resettled his hard hat, jaw set. "So?"

Sam shrugged. "I just figured you might be going up there to give her an update on the bear situation at the dump."

"Hadn't planned on it," he said gruffly, glowering straight ahead. Curtis Winthrop—*Doctor* Curtis Winthrop—could do anything he damned well pleased. Maybe he'd go walking on the mountain and run into old Lucifer. Slate smiled malevolently, luxuriating in the fantasy for a moment or two.

"Quite a woman, isn't she?"

Slate gave a noncommittal grunt.

"Man would be a damned fool to let a woman like that get away from him."

"You up here on business, or just wastin' time I haven't got?"

"I hear he buys her flowers. Those fancy hothouse things you get in the city. Heard they can run a buck or more a bloom."

Slate gave a derisive snort. "More money than brains, then. What the hell would she want flowers for? Whole damn mountain's in bloom. All she'd have to do is step outside."

"Some women like flowers."

For some reason, Slate found himself thinking of pink, lacy underwear. *Lingerie*, Curtis would call it. Hell, maybe he even bought it for her. Sounded like the kind of man who'd enjoy buying women's underwear. "Suppose he buys her perfume, too."

"I doubt it," Sam said thoughtfully. "She told me once she never wears it—got to do with the way it affects the bears or something. Makes them aggressive."

He'd never thought about it before, but Sam was right: he'd never caught even a hint of bottled scent on her. Her own perfume was heady enough, an evocative woman smell that always made him think of fresh air, green grass and mountains.

"I figure a man would be safe with flowers," Sam said after lengthy deliberation.

"Winch cable," Slate said half to himself. "She said something about needing a new winch cable."

"*Winch* cable?" Sam stared at Slate in disbelief. "No damned wonder you're still single! You have definitely been in the bush too long, McCall. We're talking about *courting* a woman, not hiring her to skid logs!"

"*I* wasn't talking about courting anything," Slate said heatedly. "Don't you have anything to do?"

"A kitten, maybe." Sam's face brightened. "Yeah, that's an idea! Women love kittens."

"*Now* what are you talking about?"

"A gift, McCall," Sam said patiently. "Something for Jamie when you go up there this weekend."

"I am not going to see Jamie this weekend," Slate enunciated with precision. "And I've got better things to do than stand out here listening to you rabbiting on about Winthrop and . . . flowers!" He turned and strode across to his own trailer.

"Man's gotta take a stand sometime," Sam yelled after him. "Look what it did for *us* at the Little Big Horn!"

In his own trailer a few minutes later, Slate was still thinking about Winthrop. He tossed his hard hat onto the desk and poured himself a cup of coffee, eyes narrowed as he took a swallow. Flowers. How the hell could a man compete with someone who bought *flowers*? Well, to hell with it. He wasn't going up there. No way he was going to make a fool out of himself just to get a good look at Jamie Kilpatrick's anthropologist. No way.

Three days later, Slate still hadn't gotten Curtis Winthrop out of his mind. It was driving him crazy, thinking of him up there with her. He was probably stretched out in that big easy chair in front of the fire with his feet up, a glass of good brandy at his elbow and a pipe in his hand. Jamie would be curled up on the floor in front of him, head resting on his knee as she stared into the flames. Her hair would be loose and Winthrop would reach out now and again to run his fingers through it.

"Damn it!" Slate lunged to his feet and paced to the open door of his office. He stood looking at the dam for a minute or two, then paced back to his desk. He eyed the stacks of paperwork waiting to be done, then swore again and wheeled toward the door.

He set out with no destination in mind, just walking hard and fast to work up a good sweat. Hands jammed in his jacket pockets, head down, he ignored anyone who called out to him, pretending to be on urgent business.

He found himself on the mountain slope just above where the dam joined the natural rock without even remembering climbing the steep path to get there. There were a few patches of grass up here, clumps of colorful wildflowers, and the breeze was warm and scented of pine. Slate sat down and stretched his legs out, relaxing back on his elbows, and gazed at the top of the dam just below him without seeing a thing.

A tuft of bluebells danced in the breeze by his foot. He looked at them, feeling a tiny jab of jealousy as he thought of Curtis Winthrop and his hothouse flowers.

How the hell could he compete with someone like that? He couldn't remember the last time he'd bought a woman flowers. Couldn't remember the last time he'd deliberately set out to woo a woman. He'd always just let things take their natural course. If it worked out, fine; if it didn't, well, that was fine, too.

Then again, he'd never met a woman like Jamie Kilpatrick before, either.

Damn. Maybe Sam was right and he *had* been out on the fringes of civilization for too long. And maybe Dave's wife was right, too, when she warned him that he was turning into one of those odd old geezers you found in the mountains talking to trees and wearing last year's long johns.

A man would be a damned fool to let a woman like that get away....

The bluebells seemed to nod in agreement.

He swore at them and got to his feet abruptly, then stood with hands on hips and stared unseeing at the dam. Something had happened to him over the past few weeks. Ever since he'd tumbled headlong into that trap of Jamie's, he'd sensed a change within himself, acknowledged it without understanding what it meant or where it would lead him. It had made him restless and edgy, and for the first time in his life he found himself filled with doubts: about his life, his future, decisions he'd made, those he had yet to make.

And it was all wrapped up somehow with a redheaded, green-eyed witch called Jamie Kilpatrick.

This past week had been hell. He'd been torn between wanting to be with her and wanting to keep her out of his life, telling himself twenty times a day that there was no future in it, that a love affair at this point was just an added complication he didn't need. That the only thing he could afford to have on his mind for the next eighteen months was the dam, and he had neither the time nor the energy to put into a relationship.

Relationship. Wasn't that the next step up from "love affair" and just a step away from white picket fences and lawn mowers? All the things he'd decided he'd never have?

Damn. He drew in a deep breath and stared up at the sky. Was this it? Was this what falling in love felt like? God, it had been so long he couldn't even remember. So many years of filling his life with what he thought mattered, only to find himself wondering if it had mattered at all.

Maybe it was time for Slater McCall to come in from the cold.

He smiled a little grimly. If that's what he truly wanted, then he'd better be prepared to fight for it. He had not only Curtis Winthrop to contend with, but Jamie's fears as well. It might take a long, long time.

But then again, he had the rest of his life.

Man's gotta take a stand sometime.

And suddenly, he realized there'd never been any doubt. Once made, the decision seemed ridiculously easy and he wondered how he'd ever thought it could be otherwise. Smiling, he turned and headed back down the slope.

Something made him pause and look back at the bluebells. He gave a snort and turned away. Took three strides. Stopped. Looked around at the flowers again.

Then he sighed and walked back. He looked down at them uncomfortably. Then, glancing around to make sure no one was watching, he reached down and gave them a pull.

They came free of the damp soil effortlessly and he started to smile before realizing things weren't quite right. Dismayed, he stared at the dangling, muddy roots. Is this what a man had to go through to court a woman these days? He muttered an oath at Sam Two Elks. Compared with this, putting a dam across a mountain river was child's play!

It was only then that he remembered he was still in full view of the entire site and he hastily stuffed the flowers into his jacket pocket, roots and all. He'd trim them up later. All it would take was one wise guy to spot him up here picking flowers, and he'd never hear the end of it.

"I don't understand why you're being so stubborn." Curtis brushed the knee of his slacks peevishly. "Dog hair. Every time I come up here, I get covered with dog hair. I don't understand why you allow that animal in the house.

In fact," he added darkly, "at times I don't understand *you*, Jameison."

Jamie fought down an urge to scream. "I simply said I hadn't made up my mind yet," she said very calmly.

"And I simply said we should consider getting an estimate on what the property might bring. *If* we decide to sell."

"If *I* decide to sell," Jamie said with a slight edge. Curtis gave her a sharp look and she sighed. "Curtis, this mountain meant everything to my father. It's all he had; it's all I have of him. Selling it is so...final."

"You can't hang on to memories forever. In another year, you won't even recognize this valley. There'll be a lake out there where the river is now, the place will be full of tourists and fishermen. The people who want to buy this mountain are willing to pay top dollar for it. Procrastinate much longer, and they'll find some other, less idealistic landowner and buy from him."

"I'm not being idealistic. I just don't like the idea of seeing Skookum Mountain turned into a fat farm!"

"I've told you a dozen times," he said in that tone of exaggerated patience parents use with troublesome children, "that High Country Resort is *not* a fat farm. It's a reducing clinic and luxury health spa that caters to a very exclusive clientele."

"A very *expensive* fat farm," she conceded.

He ignored her. "It's not as though you need it. After we're married, you won't be coming up here anymore."

Jamie looked away, trying not to let him see the unhappiness on her face. She hated to admit it, but he was right. It wasn't exactly fitting for the newly appointed associate professor of anthropology to be married to a woman who spent her summers rolling around in the dirt tagging bears. She'd publish the results of her four-year study, take a junior teaching position and spend her spare hours learning the politics and strategies required of a woman who would one day be wife of the department head. "I know," she whispered, staring into the flames. "It's just..." She shrugged, not even knowing how to express the desolation that swept over her whenever she thought of selling the Mountain.

"It's not as though we couldn't use the money," Curtis reminded her.

"Well, that's another thing." Jamie paused, choosing her words carefully. "Curtis, I'm not convinced we should go ahead with the plans to expand our study area. We've got six traps out there now, and over two dozen camera installations, and—"

"And we haven't caught a thing," Curtis completed for her. He leaned forward, eyes and face intense. "Using the information your father put together, we have an opportunity to discover an entirely new species of life! The expanded setup *is* expensive. So is the four-man research team I want to put together to back it up. But if I'm going to succeed, I've got to put two hundred percent effort into it. That means more traps, more cameras, and a fully equipped exploration team to comb these mountains one tree at a time, if necessary. Damn it, Jameison, you know how important this is to me! Those things do exist out here—and I'm going to be the person who proves it!"

As it always did, Curtis's fierce urgency made Jamie uncomfortable. Ever since meeting her father two years earlier, he'd become as obsessed as Ben had been with proving that Sasquatch exist. But there were times a tiny niggle of doubt made her wonder if his fervor was honest scientific curiosity, or just part of his desperate need to compete with his own father.

She got to her feet and wandered to the big window overlooking the valley. Curtis came up behind her a moment later and slipped his arm around her waist. "What's the matter, darling? You've been in a strange mood all weekend."

Jamie moved out of his loose embrace, restless. "I just can't help thinking that my father wouldn't like what we're doing here. How we're using his research. His money, if I sell the Mountain to finance a major search." She turned to look at him. "He didn't believe in intrusive research, Curtis. He wanted to study these creatures in their natural habitat, not mount an expedition to hunt them down."

"I intend to give him credit, if that's what you're worrying about."

"That's not what I'm worrying about," she said irritably, feeling a twinge of guilt as she realized the thought had occurred to her. "It's just that—" She broke off as Timber suddenly jumped up barking. He raced toward the kitchen door, ears cocked, then he started gyrating and whimpering with excitement as someone walked across the veranda.

"It must be Sam." Relieved at the interruption, Jamie walked to the door, nudging the delighted dog out of the way with her knee so she could open it. "Hi, I wondered if—" She swallowed the rest of her greeting with a gasp of surprise as she found herself face-to-face with Slate McCall.

"Hi." He grinned down at her through the screen door. "Got a few minutes?"

Her heart gave a somersault as those laughing golden eyes met hers and she suddenly felt a little breathless and warm. "Well, I . . ." She glanced over her shoulder. Curtis was standing by the window, his expression still impatient. "I . . . I guess so."

She stepped back to let him in and nearly fell over Timber. The dog shouldered by her with a yelp of greeting and started prancing playfully as Slate stepped through the door. Laughing, he started wrestling with the big dog and the two of them staggered into the kitchen in a flurry of laughter and mock growling, Timber as exuberant as a pup.

Curtis turned away from the window and watched the two of them curiously, eyes cool. "Jameison?"

"Oh, I'm sorry. Timber, settle down!" She grabbed the dog by his collar and hauled him back onto all fours. "This is Slater McCall, project engineer down at the dam. Slate, this is—"

"Dr. Curtis Winthrop," Slate said with a broad grin, walking across and shoving his hand out. "Heard a lot about you."

"Really?" Curtis looked at the hand distastefully.

Slate laughed and wiped it on his jeans. "Sorry. Dog drools when he's excited."

"Yes, he does seem to...like you." Curtis shook the proffered hand, surreptitiously wiping his palm with his handkerchief a moment later. Jamie glared at him, but Slate didn't seem to notice.

No one said anything. Slate had lounged back against the dining-room table, long legs crossed, arms folded on his chest, and was looking at Curtis interestedly. Curtis eyed him back, and Jamie could feel sudden tension start to build. She looked from one to the other of them with growing astonishment as she began to realize what was going on. She'd seen the same thing take place between sexually mature bears often enough to recognize it when it was happening right in her own living room. With bears, a lot of muscle flexing and verbal aggression would follow, each trying to outintimidate the other.

"Mr. McCall, would you like some coffee?" She stepped between the two of them smoothly, giving Slate a glare that made him grin broadly. "Although I wouldn't want to keep you...."

"Sounds great." His gaze held hers a moment longer than it needed to, and Jamie could sense Curtis shifting uneasily behind her as he caught the unmistakable intimacy between them. Slate pushed himself away from the table and strolled into the kitchen, getting himself a mug from the cupboard and pouring a cup of coffee with the air of a man very much at home. He looked at Curtis and held the pot up questioningly.

"No, thank you." Curtis's tone was clipped and he gave Jamie a hard look. "Mr. McCall is a friend of yours, I gather."

"The name's Slate," his rival said with an easy smile. Sauntering into the living room and settling into the easy chair that Curtis had obviously just vacated, Slate set his feet up on the hassock and smiled contentedly. "Say, Irish, that's quite a flat tire you've got on the Jeep out there. I'll take a couple of minutes and change it for you, if you like."

"Flat tire?" Curtis looked at her. "What flat tire?"

"I just noticed it this morning," she replied quietly. "I must have picked up a nail last night. I'll change it later."

"It's a hell of a messy job," Slate said. "Jeep's so covered with mud I hardly recognize it. I'll change it before I leave."

"We appreciate the offer, McCall," Curtis said tightly, "but I'll change it for her."

"Curtis, I drove up the logging road before you got here yesterday, and the Jeep is filthy. There's no rush."

"She's right," Slate put in pleasantly. His gaze wandered over Curtis's perfectly tailored slacks and oatmeal-coloured sport jacket. "You're not exactly dressed for it." He grinned lazily. "Changing Jeep tires is a little more up my alley."

"I said I'll change it," Curtis said through clenched teeth.

"For heaven's sake," Jamie exclaimed angrily, "I'm perfectly capable of changing the damned tire myself!"

Slate gave a rumbling laugh. "I don't doubt that at all, Irish. I admire a woman who can take care of herself, but a man's got his pride. Call it chivalry if you like, but I figure a man who'd let a lady change a Jeep tire herself isn't much of a man."

Jamie fixed him with a scorching glare, but before she could say anything Curtis was taking off his jacket. "I'll do it right now," he said briskly, rolling up his sleeves. "You should have mentioned it earlier, Jameison."

She stared at him. "Curtis, don't be an idiot! You'll get covered with mud. And besides, you've never changed a truck or Jeep tire in your life!"

It was, Jamie realized instantly, the wrong thing to say. Curtis flushed, his mouth going hard and thin.

"It'd be a shame to ruin those nice pants," Slate drawled from the depths of the easy chair. "Why don't you leave it, Winthrop. I've been changin' truck tires all my life. I can have it off and a new one on in no time flat."

"I realize your background may give you an edge on practical application, McCall," Curtis told him pleasantly, "but I'm sure someone with advanced degrees in anthropology and social history can manage to figure out how to change a tire."

Outraged by Curtis's rudeness, Jamie had her mouth open to jump to Slate's defence before she realized she'd nearly fallen into the same trap that Curtis had. "Curtis," she said in a conciliatory tone, "please don't bother to—"

The bang of the kitchen door interrupted her as he stalked out. Slate eased himself to his feet, grinning a self-satisfied grin, and Jamie turned on him. "What do you think you're doing?" she asked in a ferocious whisper. "Now he's going to go out there and make a fool of himself trying to prove he's as macho as you are! God, you men make me so *furious* with your stupid little games!"

"The man's old enough to take care of himself," Slate drawled. "You look great, by the way." His gaze took in her casual khaki skirt and black tank top appreciatively. "First time I've seen you out of jeans." The grin widened. "Well, not the first time, exactly, but—"

"Don't you even *think* it," Jamie hissed, cheeks burning. "Now you go out there and help that man before he kills himself trying to prove he's tougher than you are!"

Curtis had managed to get the Jeep jacked up by the time they got outside, and he gave Slate a look of smug triumph. Still sipping his coffee, Slate leaned his shoulder against one of the veranda posts and watched benignly. "Do you want a hand getting it off the axle? Looks like it's stuck on there mighty tight."

"I can handle it." Curtis gave the wheel a tug, trying not to brush against the mud-coated fender. It didn't budge, and he gave it another pull, harder this time.

"They can be tricky," Slate said helpfully.

Curtis ignored him, taking a firmer grip on the muddy tire and wrenching it toward him. It gave a little and he smiled, flashing Slate a disdainful look.

"You've got the jack set on pretty soft ground," Slate said mildly.

Curtis muttered something Jamie didn't quite catch and gave the tire a tremendous pull, and in the next moment he was flat on his back with the muddy tire cradled on his chest. He was on his feet in an instant, swearing ferociously as he looked down at his shirt and slacks. He went to wipe at them, realized his hands were in worse condition than his clothing, and swore again.

"You might want to kind of work it loose next time," Slate suggested. "Not as quick, maybe, but easier on the clothes."

Curtis's usually neatly combed hair had fallen over his forehead and he gave it an impatient swipe with his muddy hand, then realized what he'd done and swore a third time, scrubbing furiously at his face with his arm. "Where the hell's the spare?" he demanded, his face red.

"I think it's that lump lashed onto the grill," Slate said, gesturing toward the Jeep's mud-encrusted front with his coffee mug. "Don't take this the wrong way, Winthrop, but if it was me, I'd toss a couple of buckets of water over it first."

"I don't need your advice," Curtis said savagely.

"I'll get it," Jamie said swiftly.

"And I don't need *your* help, either!" Curtis practically shouted at her. The rope securing the spare was all but lost in the mud covering the grill, but Curtis poked around until he found the loose end and started pulling it free.

"I'd watch the jack, if I were you," Slate said curtly.

"Just mind your damned business, McCall!"

"Curtis, it's—" Jamie held her breath as the jack suddenly skidded and the Jeep crashed soundly onto the front left axle.

"Oh, for—!" Nearly apoplectic with rage, Curtis threw the spare tire onto the ground. "I know when I've been set up!" he shouted at Jamie as he strode by her. "Get Tarzan to change the damned thing, because I'm through being made a fool of!"

It was interesting, Slate mused, to watch the play of colors across Winthrop's thin, handsome face. Jamie's color had risen, too, and he watched her fight the obvious urge to throw something at the back of Winthrop's head as he stalked toward the cabin. He shouldered by Slate without a word, earning a soft growl from Timber, and pulled the screen door open.

It slammed behind him and Slate took another swallow of coffee to hide his smile. Jamie stopped at the bottom of the steps and Slate gazed down at her. "So that's Curtis."

"Ohhh, I'd like to—" She stamped up the steps and walked by him, giving him a look that could have cut glass.

Slate simply took another swallow of coffee and stayed where he was, enjoying the late afternoon sun. He heard voices after a moment or two, angry impatient voices that got progressively angrier and more impatient over the next couple of minutes. There was silence after a while, then Jamie's quiet voice, too low for him to hear what she said.

A moment later, Curtis came charging out, cleaner now but no less furious. He strode toward the car and threw his briefcase into the back seat, then pulled the driver's door open, pausing long enough to glare up at Slate. "You want her, McCall?" he shouted, "then, by God, you can damned well have her!"

He backed the car out so recklessly he sent a stack of firewood flying, then he rammed it into gear and floored the accelerator, spraying dirt and pine needles as he fishtailed out of the yard and down the narrow road.

Jamie was on the veranda in the next instant, her cheeks scarlet, and she stared after the rapidly disappearing car with an expression of exasperated anger.

"Interesting fellow," Slate said mildly. "A bit excitable, maybe, but—"

"Oh . . . damn you!" She glared up at him, eyes blazing.

"Me?" Slate asked innocently. "I just came up to talk to you about your bears, and—"

"You deliberately goaded him into this...this stupid display of macho—" Her eyes narrowed. "What about my bears?"

He shrugged, grinning. "Nothing in particular. I just figured that since I haven't seen you for a few days, I'd get caught up on how things are going out at the dump."

"Everything's just fine at the dump," she assured him furiously, "and everything *used* to be fine here, too!" She flung her arms out, gesturing at the scattered firewood, her Jeep. "Look at this mess."

"Why don't you go and make a fresh pot of coffee while I finish changing that tire," Slate told her calmly. Not waiting for her reply, he started rolling up his shirtsleeves and walked toward the Jeep.

It took him nearly half an hour to change the tire and restack the firewood, and when he came back in, Jamie was sitting in her father's chair. She ignored him as he went into the bathroom to wash up. She was still ignoring him five minutes later when he came out.

He strolled across to the fireplace and leaned one elbow on the mantel, looking down at her. "I lied. I didn't come up here to talk about your bears. I came up here to talk about us."

"Us?" She was on her feet again, pacing angrily. "There is no 'us,' McCall."

"Jamie, I told you once that I don't play games. I don't make promises I don't intend to keep, I don't tell a woman I love her because I think it's what she wants to hear—and I don't make love to a woman just because I think I can. I'm not the kind of man who *needs* a woman in his life to feel like a man, but damn it, Jamie, when one comes around who makes me feel the way you do, I'm not going to back down and give her up without a fight."

"A fight?" She looked around at him in astonishment. "Is that what this was all about?"

"Is Winthrop going to be back?"

"My God, you men drive me crazy! You get into this...this classic sexual-aggression thing and suddenly you're acting like cavemen!"

"I asked you about Winthrop," Slate said stubbornly. He was going to get the truth out of her if they had to stand here all night.

Jamie shot him a furious look. "He thinks you and I are 'involved,' as he put it. He's furious."

"Is that what the two of you were arguing about in here?"

Her angry glare faltered, broke. She looked out the window. "He told me that unless I went back to Seattle with him today, he was calling it off between us."

Slate gazed at her back for a long while. "And you told him you were staying."

"Of course I'm staying." She looked at him as though astounded that he even had to ask. "I've put four years of my life into those bears out there. I'm not going to throw all that away just because Curtis is acting like an idiot."

"That idiot," Slate reminded her, "is the man you were planning to marry. Where does that stand now?"

"I don't know," she retorted impatiently. "McCall, will you stop interrogating me! This has got nothing to do with you."

"It's got everything to do with me," he said flatly. "It's got to do with what happened at the hot spring, and it's got to do with what's happening between us right now."

"Nothing's happening between us!" She knew she was lying even as she shouted it, knew whatever strange magic had brought them together at the hot spring was as strong and vital as ever. It made her feel trapped and smothered and out of control, and she spun away from him, away from those burning amber eyes that could see thoughts as clearly as printed words. "What happened at the spring was an accident, I already told you that. A...a whim."

"We didn't make love at the spring because of any whim, and you damned well know it." His voice was low and intense. "We've got something here, Jamie. Something real.

I don't even pretend to understand it, and for a while that drove me crazy. That's the engineer in me, the part of me that has to know all the answers, that doesn't believe a thing exists unless I can measure it or find a mathematical formula for it or hold it in my hands. But what I feel for you *is* real, I'm starting to accept that. It's as real as what I see in your eyes when you look at me. As real as you were in my arms the other afternoon.''

"No!" She clamped her hands over her ears, trying to shut him out.

"What are you so frightened of, Jamie?" His voice was just a purr of sound, so close that Jamie had to catch her breath.

It took her every ounce of willpower to stay where she was. Every instinct she had was screaming at her to bolt for safety, yet she knew she had to hold her ground. Like old Lucifer, if Slate sensed even the slightest weakening, he'd be in for the kill. He was standing so close to her she could swear she felt his breath on the back of her neck.

"Why do you keep fighting me when you know it's what we both want?" he murmured. Even braced for it, the touch of his mouth on her throat made her flinch. "Stop fighting it, Jamie. Just let go. Let me love you the way I want to love you." His hands settled on her shoulders and he moved his mouth slowly to her ear, the tip of his tongue tracing a trail of fire up the side of her throat. Tiny spangles of liquid heat spilled through her and Jamie closed her eyes, fighting the temptation to simply turn and lose herself in his embrace, the lovemaking that was sure to follow. "I've never felt this way about a woman before, Jamie," he whispered. He nuzzled the sensitive spot under her ear, his tongue moving slyly. "You do things to me I've only dreamed of. I want you . . . I want you more than I've ever wanted anything in my life."

Ten

Where the strength came from, Jamie had no idea, but she somehow managed to keep her face turned resolutely away from his. "You don't want me," she said in a tight whisper, "you just want the challenge. That's what men like you live for, McCall—the battle of wills. Whether you're fighting a river or a mountain or a woman, it's the fight you love. But once we're tamed—once that river is dammed and controlled, once I'm so much in love with you I'm crazy with it—you'll be gone, looking for the next one."

His fingers tightened on her shoulders and she could feel the sudden tension in him, the impatience. "That's not what you're afraid of, Jamie. Hell, that would be easy—no ties, no commitment, just a few months of easy sex with a man who'd never expect anything else." He drew his hands from her shoulders in a lingering caress and stepped around to look down at her, gaze holding hers intently. "What scares you is the truth—that I *do* want it all. You, that house with the white picket fence, kids, the whole damned thing. You're just plain scared to let someone love you, Jamie, because the only kind of love you know is the kind with strings attached—the kind your parents gave you.''

"My parents loved me!''

"Sure, they loved you. But it was conditional love, Jamie. They used your love to get at each other. Your mother's still using it, using your fear of losing her love to manipulate you into living the kind of life she always wanted. Maybe she really believes she's saving you from a lot of hurt, but that's not what it's about. It's about winning and losing, Jamie. If she can blackmail you into leaving this mountain and the bears and everything you love up here, she's won. She can finally say that she was right and that you loved her best, after all.''

"That's crazy,'' Jamie whispered, turning away. Her heart was pounding and she felt that smothering feeling of childhood panic closing in around her again. "Please, I...I want you to leave.''

"Doing what *you* want to do with your life doesn't mean choosing between them, Jamie. And love doesn't have to come with trade-offs and terms attached. Love doesn't mean having to give up one thing to get another.''

Jamie said nothing, too numb and stiff to even move. There was a long, taut silence, then she heard him swear ferociously under his breath and stalk across to the door.

"I love you, Jamie,'' he said, so quietly she wondered for a moment if she'd merely imagined it. "And I think you love me, too, except you're too damned scared to admit it.''

She ached to turn around, to look at him, but she felt as though she'd turned to glass. One wrong move and she'd shatter into a million bright bits, and there wouldn't be enough of her left for anyone. She heard the door open. And then, after another long silence, it closed with a bang.

His footsteps crossed the veranda, sharp with anger, and Jamie watched from the window as he strode down the steps and across to his truck. He shoved his hand into his jacket pocket and brought out the keys, but instead of getting into the truck he paused. Frowning, he reached into his pocket again and drew something out that looked like a handful of grass. He looked at it for a long moment, then up at the cabin. Then, almost wearily, he tossed whatever it was onto the ground and turned away. He got into the truck and a moment or two later she watched as it drove away, brake lights flickering as he rounded the sharp corner and disappeared.

He was gone.

It was what she wanted. Jamie swallowed, her throat thick and aching. Damn it, it was what she'd wanted!

For some reason, she found her gaze drawn back to the little bundle of grass lying on the ground where he'd discarded it. Still too numb to really feel anything yet, she walked outside and down the veranda steps, then knelt down and picked up the tattered, crumpled little bouquet of flowers.

"Bluebells." Her voice cracked and she had to blink as her eyes suddenly swam with tears. She stared at the tiny flowers wonderingly, feeling the crystal ache within her start to fracture and break. She tried to smile but her chin kept wobbling so badly she couldn't. She could see him up there on the mountainside, gruff and embarrassed, telling himself he was being ten kinds of fool even as he pulled them up, praying all the while that no one was watching him. But he'd done it anyway. Because he'd known they'd make her smile. Because he loved her....

"Oh, Slate!" The tears were impossible to stop now. They trickled down her cheeks and she suddenly realized she was sobbing. "I love you."

But it was too late now.

A guttural rumble of thunder rolled down the valley, seeming to shake the very air. Echoes boomed off the mountain ramparts across the river and Slate glanced at the sky. It was still clear, sprinkled with early stars. The storm was moving into the valley from the north, the hulking mass of indigo clouds shot through with flickers of lightning. The air had already turned cool and still and even the giant pines sheltering his trailer seemed listless, their big boughs drooping.

It was going to be a mountain rattler, all right. Standing in the door of his trailer, one shoulder braced against the frame, Slate lifted the bottle to his lips and took a long swallow of beer. Maybe it was what they all needed. The weather had been sultry and unsettled all week and everyone seemed edgy and restless.

He took another long swallow of beer, letting the cool liquid trickle down his throat. Another rumble of thunder muttered down the valley and a puff of cool wind made the pines whisper. Unable to stop himself, he let his glance slip northward. The rounded, tree-tufted silhouette of Skookum Mountain stood against the sky, black on black. Dark clouds were already spilling around its upper crags and even as he watched, a silver curtain of rain swept over the crest, veiling it from sight.

Was she standing at the window, watching the storm sweep toward her? Did she find her gaze drawn helplessly southward even as his was drawn again and again toward her? Did she find herself thinking about him even while fighting not to, her mind so filled with every detail of his face, his voice, the sound of his laugh that she wondered if she was going a little mad?

No! Damn it, no. Slate pushed himself away from the door frame and walked back into his trailer, kicking the door closed behind him. He wasn't going to drive himself crazy like that. He'd put himself on the line up there today—and it hadn't worked out. He could either spend the rest of his life brooding about what might have been, or he could admit he'd been a damned fool to ever think it was possible and get on with building this dam.

He pulled the fridge open and reached for another bottle of beer without thinking about what he was doing, then caught himself and slammed it closed again with a soft oath. That wasn't the answer, either.

There was no answer, except maybe time and hard work. Neither would erase the pain, but, given long enough, they'd dull it to a bearable level. The sense of loss was the worst, which was ridiculous, given he'd never *had* her to lose. Or maybe it wasn't the loss of Jamie herself as much as the loss of the dream, the hope that maybe this time it was his to capture, his to have.

Which only proved the old adage about there being no fool quite like an old one.

"Damn it!" He slammed his fist against the fridge door and wheeled around, grabbed up the kettle and started to fill it, then tossed it aside again. On the radio behind him a bourbon-voiced woman was singing about lost loves and broken dreams, and he swore under his breath and strode into his small living room. He switched on the TV and flung himself onto the sofa, was on his feet a few moments later, pacing, as restless as a cat.

The wind had picked up, blowing in fitful gusts that made the trailer windows rattle. He could hear the surf sound of the big pines, the scrape of a bough on the roof and then, finally, the first patters of rain. He stared out the window above the sink but it was too dark to see much of anything. He could catch a glimpse of the floodlit dam through wind-tossed branches, the outline of his mud-spattered truck parked nearby. The rest of the valley was lost behind a curtain of falling rain and as he watched, it swept over the dam, all but obliterating it from view, and a few moments later the patter of rain on the metal roof turned to a staccato drumbeat.

The window rattled as a sheet of wind-blown rain hit it and Slate turned away, wishing he'd gone down to the main camp before the storm had hit. The big recreation center down there had a weight room and he could do with a good workout to burn off some of this tension and restlessness. And a long cold shower probably wouldn't hurt, either.

He gave his head a slow shake. God, he was in sorry shape! He was thirty-seven years old and no stranger to the world. He'd worked in some of the worst hellholes on earth, fighting river and mountain, drought and flood. He'd seen good men die, and in a mercifully brief descent into that nightmare called Vietnam, he'd even killed. He'd been married and divorced. He was familiar with the rituals of love, if not with love itself. And yet, in the space of three short weeks, this green-eyed vixen had brought him to his knees.

And damn it, he loved her. Even now, even knowing she wouldn't have him, he loved her.

He hadn't fully realized it himself until he'd said the words aloud just as he'd left her cabin. He'd never found them easy to say, yet they'd fit as comfortably on his tongue today as his own name.

The lights went out at that moment, leaving him standing in utter darkness. Sighing, he reached over and turned off the silent radio, then made his way into the living room and shut off the television as well. He switched off what lights he could remember had been burning, then dropped wearily onto the sofa again and stretched out full-length and watched flickers of lightning play across the ceiling without really seeing anything at all.

He wakened with a start, heart pounding, trying to remember where he was. The trailer was still dark except for the occasional flash of lightning. He yawned and rubbed his eyes and was about to sit up when another flicker of lightning lit the room and, in that time-held instant, Jamie's face appeared beside him, so real it made him catch his breath.

He froze, too startled to do more than stare blindly into the darkness, eyes still seared by the flash of lightning. God, he was losing his mind. Or was still asleep and dreaming. As his eyes adapted to the darkness, he found himself staring at where he'd seen the image, convinced he could make out the faint silhouette of a woman's head against the window.

Tentatively, feeling like a fool but unable to stop himself, he put out his hand.

And touched cool, wet skin.

His startled oath cracked through the room and he sat up, put his hand out again. His fingers brushed wet hair this time, thickly braided, then the curve of a cheek, the lush ripeness of a woman's mouth. The lips kissed his fingertips, curving in a smile.

"Sorry I startled you," she whispered. "I knocked, but I guess you didn't hear me over the rain and thunder."

"Jamie!" Scarcely even daring to believe he was awake, he touched her face again, her features invisible but so familiar he needed no light to know it was she. Really Jamie, not just a dream image conjured up by a desperate, heartbroken mind. "How long have you been here?"

"Just a couple of minutes. I thought you were down at the dam, so I let myself in to wait. Then I saw you lying here asleep, and I... I've been sitting here, wondering what to say."

Say you love me, he felt like shouting, but he bit it back, refusing to let himself hope. "Are you all right?"

A soft laugh emanated from the darkness. "Soaked to the skin. I ran the Jeep into a monster pothole a hundred yards up the road and had to walk the rest of the way."

Slate chuckled, still not believing she was real. "We've lost three trucks and a flatbed in that one this week alone." He swung his feet to the floor. "I'll break out the candles and find you some dry—"

"No, wait." She caught his hand in hers and he sank back onto the sofa. "It... I want to say something," she whispered, "and it's easier in the dark."

Slate's heart gave a painful lurch and he eased his breath between his teeth, bracing himself. "Jamie—"

"Please, Slate," she said softly. "I... I've been practicing this all the way down here." Slate nodded, forgetting for a moment that she couldn't see him, and folded his fingers tightly around hers. He could hear her swallow. "After you left this afternoon, I tried to convince myself that it was best that way. You scare me to death, Slate, because for the first time in my life I know what really loving someone means. What passion really means. And I always thought feeling that way about a man meant losing control of your life.''

She paused, and Slate squeezed her fingers in gentle encouragement. She cupped her other hand around his and he felt her lips brush the back of his wrist, heard her take a deep breath. ''You...you were right when you said I believed that love is a trade-off. It's always been like that in my life. I could never just have *love*—there were always strings attached. Every spring when school let out and I'd want to come up here for the summer, I'd have to go through the same song and dance with my mother—the arguments, the hurt feelings, the silent routine. She'd finally give in, but by then I'd be sick with guilt and absolutely convinced she didn't love me anymore.

''I always adored being up here with Dad, but by early September, when it was time for me to go back to school, things would get tense between us. He figured I'd learn as much at the local school as I could in Vancouver, and he and Mom would be battling it out on the phone. He'd ask me which I preferred, and of course I was terrified to come out and agree with him because I knew Mom would figure I'd finally *changed sides*, as she always put it.

''So Dad would take me back to Vancouver and he and Mom would have a fight—the kind where they were both too civilized to shout and scream in front of me, so they'd just take potshots at each other. Then Dad would finally leave. He'd pick up a case of Irish whiskey and come back to the Mountain, and he'd sit up here and drink for weeks on end and I would be sick with guilt again, feeling as though I'd abandoned him.''

She took another deep breath, this one a little unsteady. He opened his mouth to tell her she didn't have to tell him all this right now, but she put her fingers lightly across his lips and he nodded again, kissing her palm. ''It hasn't stopped, even now Dad's dead. I know Mom hates it when I'm up here. I think she's jealous of the good memories I have, or maybe she's just afraid that I love the Mountain more than I love her. She's so afraid of losing me...." Her voice faded into thoughtful silence.

As I am, Slate told her silently. How could a woman be torn in so many directions at once? And what anguish had he put her through, trying to tear her into yet another? Did he have that right?

"I used to think that love was like a birthday cake, where you have to divide it up among everyone and if you don't get the pieces all the same size, someone's going to be hurt. But I don't believe that anymore. Love is like a magic well where the more you use up, the more there is to be used."

Slate felt a drop of moisture splash the back of his hand and wondered if it was rainwater dripping off her hair or tears.

Her fingers brushed his cheek, his mouth, traced the curve of his chin. "I love you," she whispered so softly he barely heard her. "And if you meant what you said this afternoon..."

Slate held his breath. Dared, finally, to ease it out between his clenched teeth. "If you're asking if I meant it when I said I love you," he said quietly, "I did. And I do. And if you're asking if I meant it when I said I want it all— you, the white picket fence, the kids, the whole damned thing—the answer is yes again."

Her fingers tightened on his. "I'm terrified."

"If it's any consolation," he said with a soft laugh, "so am I. This falling-in-love stuff isn't something I do every day, Jamie. I thought I was in love once, but at twenty-two you don't know a hell of a lot about anything, least of all love. In all the years since, I'd convinced myself that I never was going to meet that special woman who'd make me see fireworks—until I met you. And it's been like the Fourth of July ever since."

"Oh, Slate...."

He stood up and drew her to her feet, intending to make his way into the kitchen to find the candles. But instead he drew her gently into his arms. His mouth sought hers in the dark, found it easily, and instead of looking for candles and dry clothing, he found himself kissing her.

It started out as a gentle, reassuring kiss that about halfway through turned into something else altogether. Jamie sighed and stepped nearer to him, wrapping her arms around his neck and kissing him back with enough enthusiasm to send all thoughts of candles and clothing out of his mind completely. Her tongue moved against his eloquently, a deliberate evocation of the intimacies they'd already shared, and Slate felt his body respond so strongly it made his breath catch.

He slipped her wet hunting vest off and tossed it aside and heard her breath catch as he pressed her tightly against him, mouth moving hungrily on hers. Her throat was under his mouth in the next instant, skin cool and rain slick, and he ran a line of tiny, biting kisses up to her ear.

"You can't imagine how I've wanted you," he groaned. "I can't close my eyes without seeing you, without remembering the feel of you around me. I've got the taste of you so deep I'll never be free of you!"

"I was terrified you'd send me away," she whispered. "I thought I'd ruined it all."

"My God, Jamie, I love you! How could I ever send you away? I thought I'd lost you." Her mouth was under his and he claimed it hungrily. She moved against him and he ran his hands up and down her lithe back, still half believing it was all some erotic dream and that he'd wake up in a moment and find himself alone.

He didn't remember swinging her up into his arms and carrying her into the bedroom, didn't remember anything about the next few minutes at all but drowning in the scent and taste and touch of her. The next thing he knew they were on the bed, naked, her long legs wrapped around his. There was the silken whisper of flesh against flesh, the sound of their breathing, murmurs of pleasure. Body caressed body, hands sought, found the hidden, secret places, mouths met and teased and spun magic in unimagined ways.

And then she was there for him and there was that moment of gentle pressure, an indrawn breath, the silken cleaving as he eased himself into her feminine warmth. Her hips lifted even as his swung downward, meeting, seeking, accepting him. It was surrender and conquest both, giving herself even as she took him within her, and then nothing mattered anymore but the spinning, dizzying whirlpool into which they'd willingly tumbled.

It was like making love for the first time again and yet as though they'd known each other for centuries, an erotic blend of the new and the deliciously familiar, of discovery and of perfecting what had already been discovered. It was as though he could anticipate every move and sigh of delight, knew exactly how to build pleasure onto pleasure until he and she were both lost in the wonder of each other. And at the very end, when Slate's world exploded around him in an uprush of sensation so fierce it made him cry out, he felt the last barriers around his heart break and fall away.

They lay still and entwined for a long while after those last few minutes, sharing the wordless things lovers share. Then Slate realized the rain-damp breeze blowing through the open window was uncomfortably cool and he eased the bedspread out from under them both and pulled it over them. It was only then that he realized the electricity had come back on.

The kitchen light shone in the open bedroom door and he smiled as he gazed down at Jamie. "So you are real. I kept wondering if you were just a dream."

She smiled drowsily. "Which makes me ask the obvious question. Do I show up in your dreams, like this, very often?"

"I've taken more cold showers this past week than I have in the past ten years."

Jamie laughed. "You mean they really work?"

Just thinking about it made Slate wince. "Not in the least."

"And in these dreams," Jamie murmured. "Is it always as good as tonight was?"

"Tonight exceeded any dream I've ever had." And it was true. Slate gazed down at her, still not entirely convinced she was real. What quirk of fate had made him stroll up that mountain trail that night? He could as easily have gone down to the recreation center to shoot some pool and swap lies with his buddies, or taken any one of a dozen other forest trails.

The leather thong securing her braid had come off and he unraveled the rest of her hair so it flowed across the pillow and around her shoulders in fiery ripples. "Feel better?"

"Feel fantastic," she murmured with a wicked smile.

Slate laughed. "I meant your hair."

"Hair's fine. Rest of me's fine, too. Better than fine. I tingle from head to foot." She stretched luxuriously. Smiling, she smoothed his tousled, love-damp hair off his forehead. "You didn't tell me it was going to be even better this time."

"Making love in a pool can be spectacular, but it's distracting trying to keep your head above water. I was able to concentrate on what I was doing this time."

"I noticed," she whispered. "So was I."

"I noticed." Slate's smile widened as a blush made her cheeks glow. "Do you have any idea of what it does to a man's ego to make love to a woman as responsive as you are? There were a couple of times when it took all my willpower not to throw my head back and howl with the sheer arrogance of knowing I was able to make it good for you."

"Typical male dominance behavior," Jamie teased. "It's all tied up with sexual prowess and hormones and stuff...lets the other males in the area know you're still dominant sire, and at the same time attracts other females that are ready to mate."

"This dominant sire has just one female he's interested in pleasing," Slate assured her, her smile making his heart skip a beat. "I'd make a lousy bear. Hit and run isn't my style."

"Oh, I don't know," Jamie murmured, her smile mischievous. "The actual mating process between a boar and his lady can take as long as an hour. That's not exactly hit and run."

"An *hour*? Are you serious?"

"I've got it on film."

Slate broke into a smile. "Does the University of Washington know you're using their grant money to make dirty bear films?"

"It was my dirty bear films that *got* me the grant money," she said with a laugh. "And actually, it's quite romantic. I have one pair on the film who spend all afternoon in a field down by the river, just playing and making love. And that's what it is, regardless of the clinical terms—they're doing more than simply mating. They nuzzle and hold each other, then play for a while, then make love again. They're so gentle and tender with each other that I felt guilty filming them. I had to keep reminding myself that I was a scientist, not just a voyeur."

"You're a strange woman," he teased with a soft laugh. "Filled with scientific fervor one moment and dewy-eyed romanticism the next."

"You're a fine one to talk," Jamie reminded him. "You're the one who came charging up to my cabin today like a boar grizzly defending his little patch of mountain."

Slate smiled lazily. "Glad I gave in to all those aggressive male hormones?"

"If you don't know the answer to that by now, you're hopeless," she said with a laugh. "There's something to be said for aggressive male hormones."

"I wanted you," Slate said bluntly. "I had a choice of backing down, or taking a stand. I decided to come up here and give Dr. Curtis Winthrop a run for his money just to see how serious he was."

"And if he *had* been able to change that tire? What were you going to challenge him to next? Bear wrestling?"

Slate grinned. "Actually, I'd probably have invited him outside for a good old-fashioned slugging match. Primitive, but effective."

Jamie gave a peal of laughter. She kissed him lightly on the mouth, then relaxed back against him again with a contented little sigh. "Curtis isn't really that bad a guy," she murmured a few minutes later.

"Probably not," Slate replied indulgently. He could afford to be indulgent, with the lady in question in *his* arms, still warm and sleepy from their lovemaking, and Curtis Winthrop halfway to Seattle and out of her life. Slate smiled. Hell, it was enough to make a man positively warmhearted.

Jamie smiled sleepily. No wonder her mother had warned her to stay away from passionate men. How could you ever go back to safe and solid after experiencing heaven itself? She let her gaze wander over Slate's strong features, feeling a surge of joy so deep and profound that it could only be love. "You're an odd man, McCall." He looked down and Jamie smiled drowsily at him. She smoothed his eyebrows with her fingertip, traced the angular outline of his jaw. "When I first met you, all I could see was this hard-nosed, flint-eyed dam builder who was ready to roll right over anyone who got in the way of his precious project. Watch out for that Killer McCall, people would tell me. Don't mess with him—he's worse than a rabid grizzly."

"I prefer to think of it as being single-minded," Slate said with a comfortable, lazy laugh. "A man dedicated to his job."

"You're also a bit of a fraud. Sam says there's not a man out there who wouldn't walk fire for you. That Monolith has trouble handling two or three big projects at a time because all their best people refuse to work for anyone but you."

"We're all masochists or we wouldn't be in this business."

"Uh-huh. And it's this same Killer McCall who only last week ordered a major construction change—two full years into the project, mind you—so a stand of five-hundred-year-old Sitka spruce can be saved."

Slate grinned sheepishly. "So I like trees. What can I say? Maybe I was a druid in some past life."

"You're a pushover, is what you are. Sam said when he and those two guys from the Save the Skookum Committee took you up there to look at those trees, you caved in like wet cardboard. Something about baby squirrels?"

"Baby porcupines," Slate growled. "And they didn't have anything to do with it. It made better engineering sense to move the location of that access road, that's all."

"Whatever you say." Jamie kissed him lightly. "And we won't mention the bluebells you—oh, darn!" She sat up. "They're still in the bag!" She scrambled out of bed, pausing long enough to grab a work shirt hanging on the closet doorknob and slip it on, more out of concern for the chill in the air than Slate's obviously approving gaze.

"What the hell are you doing?" he grumbled, squinting against the light from the door.

"I forgot all about them," she said over her shoulder as she hurried into the kitchen. "I'll be right back."

Slate's trailer home was small but surprisingly tidy, every inch of space used economically and well. There was very little of the normal bachelor clutter she would have expected and although the place was obviously well lived-in and comfortable, it held very few of the personal touches that would give a clue about the man himself. Or maybe that was the biggest clue right there, Jamie decided as she found a glass in the cupboard and filled it with water. Maybe he resisted making it more like a home for the simple reason that it wasn't. He was just passing through, and setting down roots would only emphasize his nomadic life when the time came to move on. Maybe it was just easier not to become too attached.

She took the bluebells from the plastic bag and moist paper towel and put them in the glass of water, then carried them into the bedroom. Slate raised himself up on one elbow and gave her such a quizzical look that she blushed. "I found them after... after you left."

"I forgot I had them." He looked mildly embarrassed. "I saw them up at the dam, and...uh...thought you might like them."

"Do you think anyone saw you?" she teased gently.

"I sure as hell hope not," he replied gruffly. "If you don't like them, you can throw them out. It won't hurt my feelings any if you—"

"I love them," she said softly. "No one's ever picked me flowers before."

"I guess Winthrop buys them, does he?" Slate muttered.

"Curtis?" Jamie laughed. "He never bought me a flower in my life! He's too practical to spend good money on something that will be dead in a week."

"Well, damn that Two Elks," Slate grumbled half to himself. "He set me up!"

"Sam did what?"

He rolled onto his back, reaching for her hand and tugging her gently down onto the bed beside him. "Nothing important. Jamie, those things are half-dead. Toss them out and I'll buy you some roses."

"Roses?" She gave him a scandalized look. "Anybody can buy a woman hothouse roses—it takes a man with real class to pick a bouquet of bluebells." She leaned over and kissed him lightly, resting her arms on his shoulders and looking into his eyes. "And you, Slater J. McCall, are definitely a man of class."

"I know a good thing when I see it, if that's what you mean." He slipped his hands under the shirt and ran them up her bare back.

"They'll be fine after a few hours in water. And it was a great idea bringing the roots, too. This way I can plant them and they'll last forever instead of just a day or two." She smiled and ran her finger down the end of his nose to his mouth, tracing the full curve of his bottom lip. "Who'd have thought that anyone as bossy, stubborn, aggravating and downright bullheaded as you are would turn out to be such an old-fashioned romantic?"

Slate grinned and nipped at the end of her finger. "And who'd have thought that anyone as impossible, argumentative, frustrating and downright *pig*headed as you are would notice?"

"We make a good couple, don't we?" Jamie laughed quietly, replacing the gently exploring finger with her mouth. Slate's lips parted and she ran her tongue along the upper one, smiled when the tip of his tongue gently met hers. "What character flaws one of us lacks, the other makes up for in spades!"

"Lady," Slate said softly, tugging the shirt up so she was all but naked, "I'd say we make just about a *perfect* couple."

He held the sheet and blanket up and Jamie slipped into the warmth gratefully, pulling the shirt over her head and tossing it aside. She lay across him, one leg drawn up over his thighs, and she sighed with pleasure as he guided his mouth down over hers and kissed her deeply and slowly. The banked embers of desire he'd already quenched so perfectly once sparked to life again, filling her with an anticipatory heat that settled low in her pelvis with breathtaking explicitness.

"Mmm..." She shifted slightly, drew her leg up between his so she was straddling his muscled thigh, caught her breath as he flexed his leg gently against her. "Oh, Slate, is...is this such a good idea?"

He laughed huskily and ran his hands down her back, pressing her tightly to him. "Best idea I've had in, oh, about half an hour." He kissed her, his tongue curling around hers, drawing it deeply into his own mouth.

"But it's so soon," Jamie protested weakly. "I mean—"

"Give me your hand," he purred.

"What are—oh!" Jamie's eyes widened as he drew her hand slowly down across the muscled slab of his stomach, then lower still to where his body was proving with graphic enthusiasm that it wasn't too soon at all. "Good heavens, Mr. McCall! Are you trying to tell me something?"

"What I'm trying to tell you, Ms. Kilpatrick, is infinitely better demonstrated than explained."

Jamie gave a throaty laugh and bent her head to kiss him. "I like a man who doesn't waste words."

He didn't waste actions, either, and a few minutes later Jamie was nearly out of her mind, her body so on fire for him that every intimate caress was exquisite torture. Gently he lifted her across him, drawing her thighs up the outside of his. Jamie moved her hips, captured him, enveloped him in one sliding, honeyed caress that seemed to go on forever. He groaned her name and she moved again, downward this time, wanting as much of him as their bodies would allow.

His gaze was locked on hers, narrowed and burning, and he caught her hips in his hands and held her tight against him. "Not yet, sweetheart. We've got hours and hours."

Jamie felt her heart cartwheel. "Hours?"

He grinned and drew her mouth down to his. "Anything your bears can do, Irish..."

Jamie laughed softly and relaxed against his chest, letting the slow, rhythmic motion of his hips rock her gently. The fierce tension within her eased slightly, promising to build to an even greater peak when they were both ready, but for the moment she was content to just lie quietly with him, his gentle movements all the more erotic for the promise they held.

"I'm going to take you to heaven and back tonight," he whispered. "As many times as you want, Irish. As many times as you need."

His low, gritty voice made Jamie's breath catch and she murmured his name, unable to keep herself from moving over him. "Don't hold back, Irish," he murmured. "Don't wait for me—we've got lots and lots of time for me to catch up. I want it perfect for you, Jamie. Perfect...."

Eleven

Jamie's pager went off just as she was getting into the shower. It startled Slate so badly he spilled scalding coffee on his hand and he swore under his breath, sucking the burn as he strode across to where she had discarded her vest the previous night. He slipped the pager out of the pocket and silenced it, then tossed it on the coffee table and went back into the kitchen.

The glassful of bluebells was sitting in the middle of the table and he smiled, silently thanking whatever whim had made him pick them. Who would have thought that a handful of wilted bluebells could make such a difference in a man's life?

Jamie appeared a few minutes later, still rubbing her thick hair with a towel. She'd put on her denim shirt and pink lacy briefs but hadn't bothered with her jeans, and Slate grinned at the delectable sight she provided as she leaned across the table to pick up a slice of bacon. She was glowing from the hot water and a night of lovemaking, and her eyes danced with a thousand unworded things every time she looked at him.

He poured her a mug of coffee and handed it to her, pausing long enough to kiss her before returning to a pan of scrambled eggs. "You know, I was wondering," he said as she leaned against the counter beside him, "how would you feel about getting married in that old log church in Pine Lake? It's not very big, but the grove of trees it's set in is like a cathedral—if the weather cooperates, we could have the whole thing outside. Then—" The expression on her face stopped him cold. "What?"

Jamie was looking up at him in amused exasperation. Her lips formed a slow smile around the slice of bacon. "McCall, what am I going to do with you?" He gazed down at her blankly, and she shook her head. "Are you asking me to marry you?"

He stared at her, frowning. "I thought we'd already settled that."

Laughing, Jamie leaned forward and kissed his cheek. "Spiritually, yes. But McCall—a woman likes to be asked."

Slate stared at her a moment longer, then grinned sheepishly. "Guess I could have handled that a little better," he acknowledged, then winced. "You want the whole routine? Down on my knee, a ring...the *works*?"

Jamie's peal of laughter rang through the trailer and she slipped her arms around his neck. "You win. I'll consider myself proposed to, all right? After all, you brought me bluebells, and last night you loved me in ways a woman only dreams of being loved. That's more than I ever expected to have."

Slate gazed down at her, his chest pulling so tight he could hardly breathe. How in God's sweet name had he gotten so lucky? He kissed the end of her nose, then reached across to pick up a rubber washer from the clutter on top of the fridge. "Enough of this horsing around. If a man's going to do something, he should do it properly." Gently he slipped the washer onto the third finger of her left hand. It fit perfectly. "Jamie Kilpatrick, will you marry me?"

Biting her lip to keep from laughing, Jamie nodded seriously. "I would be honored to marry you, Slater McCall. For better or worse, thick or thin, leaky faucets—" she held up her hand "—and all."

"Kiss me."

"You," Jamie murmured as she proceeded to do just that, "have got to be the bossiest man I've ever met."

"Considering you never listen to a word I say," he reminded her, "it shouldn't be a problem." When he lifted his mouth from hers long minutes later, Slate's breathing was decidedly unsteady. "I hope you're not going to insist on a fashionably long engagement."

"Long enough to make the arrangements."

"Day after tomorrow?" He laughed at the expression on her face. "A couple of months won't kill me, I guess." Then he frowned, suddenly thinking of something. "You realize," he said carefully, "that we're not going to be able to take a honeymoon? No more than a couple of days, anyway, and even that'll have to be near a phone."

Jamie's mouth curved mischievously. "I think," she said softly, "that we've already taken care of that part of things."

"Oh, you think so, do you?" he murmured.

"Well, it was a pleasant step in the right direction," she said with a laugh. "Besides, I can't think of a better way to spend my honeymoon than right here in this trailer with you." She nipped his lower lip. "Naked." Another nip. "Not able to keep our hands off each other."

Slate's arms tightened around her. "God, I love a woman with a down-to-earth sense of priorities." He brushed his lips across hers. "I swear I'll make it up to you after this project's over. What would you say to a couple of months on a South Seas Island paradise with nothing but sand and sea and each other?"

"Will they have bears?" she asked with mock concern.

He kissed the end of her nose again. "Will pandas do? They have them in China."

"I love 'em. Are you offering me a honeymoon in China?"

Slate looked down at her, serious now. "If you had a chance to spend four years in China studying pandas, what would you say?"

"Are you serious?" Laughter rang through the words. "I'd kill for the chance! Very little is known about them, aside from the fact that they're seriously endangered because the bamboo they live on is dying as part of *its* natural cycle. But you're dreaming if you think the Chinese government is going to give a no-name ethologist from the University of Washington permission to—what are you grinning about, McCall?"

"I can't make any guarantees, but I'm fairly certain we can get that permission. We, in this case, being the U.S. government and Monolith Contractors."

Jamie's eyes narrowed. "What are you up to, McCall?"

"After this project's over, we're going to China. You, me—the whole gang. Monolith has accepted a joint-government project to build one of the biggest hydroelectric dams that part of the world has ever seen. We're going to spend four years in panda country—and I figure I can pull a few strings to get my wife permission to undertake a long-term study of the little guys."

Jamie's eyes went wide. "My God, Slate! We've got biologists over here who have been trying for *years* to get the necessary papers and clearance! There have been a couple of groups go over to work with local scientists, but...holy cow!"

"I take it that means you won't mind getting dragged off to China for four years," Slate said dryly.

"I can be packed in an hour."

"And rumor's out that we're bidding on a monster project up in northern Manitoba after that. Right on Hudson Bay."

"Northern Manitoba." She smiled blissfully. "Polar bears, McCall."

Slate had to laugh. "You're an easy woman to please, Irish. Most men have to *buy* their wives furs to get a smile like that."

"How did I get so lucky?" Arms still wrapped around his neck, she gazed up at him happily. "The man of my dreams and all the bears I can handle—what more could a lady ask for?"

"I'm the lucky one," Slate murmured.

She gave a little indrawn gasp. "What *are* you doing?"

"Seeing what you've got on under this shirt," he told her with a chuckle. "Not much, besides a bear claw and a few freckles." He pulled the shirt the rest of the way up and kissed her left breast. "You've freckles in the most intriguing places. Here, for instance. And here...."

"Slate!" Jamie gave a gasp of laughter and sank her fingers into his hair, tugging his head up. "Don't you dare start something we don't have time to finish!"

"We've got time," he purred, running his hands up under the shirt. "I don't have to be down at the dam for another hour."

Laughing, she grabbed his wrists. "Well, I don't have time. I told Terry I'd meet him at the dump at eight." She slipped out of his grasp and tugged the shirt over her bottom. "And I have to get my Jeep out of that mud hole before I can go anywhere."

Slate gave her a regretful pat on the backside and turned back to the badly overcooked eggs. "Which reminds me— you got a call while you were in the shower."

She groaned, reaching for the phone. "Who knew I was here?"

"Not the phone. Your pager." He nodded toward the coffee table.

"My pager?" The tone of Jamie's voice made Slate look around. "Do you mean it went off?"

"Yeah. Isn't that what they're supposed to do?"

She shook her head slowly, eyeing the pager as though it were dangerous. "Not that one."

"Jamie?"

"It's not a pager, exactly. It's a remote alarm, linked to the panel in my cabin." She walked to the table and picked it up. "Maybe it was just a test. Did it beep once, or—?"

"Went off like a fire bell," Slate said, walking across to her. "Jamie, what's wrong?"

She shook her head, frowning, then headed for the bedroom. "Probably nothing. But it's hooked up to the traps. And it goes off when one of them is triggered."

Slate followed her, wiping his hands on the tea towel he'd slung over his shoulder. Frowning, he watched her pull on her jeans. "You mean you've caught something? Like you caught me?"

"Exactly." She sat on the end of the bed and started pulling her boots on, glancing up at him through a tangle of hair. "Except this time it *isn't* you."

"A bear?"

"Maybe." She stuffed her shirt into her jeans and slipped between him and the door frame, worried. "Can I borrow your truck?"

"I'll drive you." Slate was perched on the arm of the chair, already pulling on his own boots. "I don't want you wandering around up there by yourself."

Jamie gave him an impatient look as she pulled on her vest. "Don't tell me husbandhood is going to turn you into a worrywart. It's going to be hard on you if you're going to build dams *and* watch over me day and night."

He grinned at her, pulling his own down-filled vest off the hook by the door. "I'll only build by day, darlin'. I intend to have you *very* close by my side at night."

But Jamie's smile was preoccupied. She fidgeted by the door while he looked for his truck keys. "We have to stop by the cabin to find out which trap it is. Slate, will you hurry!"

"In a minute." He rummaged through the closet, found the rifle case and pulled it out, then took out the heavy hunting rifle. He checked it swiftly, stopped by the kitchen long enough to grab the box of cartridges and shove it in his vest pocket. Grim faced, he stepped by Jamie and out into the crisp dawn air. "No arguments," he told her flatly. "I don't use this thing except as a last resort, but I don't mind telling you old Lucifer spooked the hell out of me the other day."

"If it's Lucifer you're worried about, don't be." She climbed into his big four-wheel-drive pickup. "He's up in the Khutzeymateen."

"Cootsey—*what*?"

"Mateen. It's a valley north of Prince Rupert that's full of grizzlies. We've been trying for years to get the government to declare it as the world's first grizzly sanctuary, but the logging companies are fighting us tooth and nail."

"And what's this got to do with Lucifer?"

"Nothing," she said with a hint of irritation. "I'm just saying that we airlifted him up there about a week ago. He came by the site dump a couple of times but got driven away—he's too old for that sort of competition. Then he started hanging around Pine Lake. We figured that sooner or later someone was going to panic and shoot the old fellow, so we took him up to the Khutzeymateen. It's ideal grizzly country, and it'll give him a chance to spend his last few years in relative comfort. He's not going to live forever, even up there, but at least he'll die a dignified death instead of being shot while eating garbage."

"And you call me a pushover," he said with a laugh. "I saw him four or five days ago out at the dam."

Jamie shook her head. "You couldn't have. Fish and Wildlife took him out two days after you and I ran into him on Skookum."

Slate looked at her. "Honey, you've got your days mixed up. I saw him after that. You sure they got the right bear?"

"I was there!"

"Well, then you've got another one out there because I was looking right at him. It was dark, but not that dark."

"Dark?" Jamie looked at him thoughtfully. "I haven't seen signs of another grizzly in the area. And they're not usually nocturnal. Although I guess it's possible." She frowned, looking even more thoughtful. "Just what did you see?"

"Something damned big! It was on the other side of the river and it stood looking down at the dam."

"Stood?"

"Up on its hind legs, like Lucifer."

"It wasn't a man?"

Slate looked at her impatiently. "If it was, he was about eight feet tall and covered in fur. Not your average tourist."

"You're sure it was a bear?"

"What else could it have been?" He gave her a sharp look. "Now don't try to convince me it was a Sasquatch, because—"

"I simply said it couldn't have been Lucifer."

Slate glanced at her but she'd subsided into a thoughtful silence and was staring out the windshield with a faint frown. There was no point in arguing with her. But if she was right about when Lucifer had been shipped up to the Khutzeymateen, then what *had* he seen that night at the dam?

It took nearly two hours to get out to the trap. It was the most isolated of the six, the road into it little more than a bone-rattling trail, and by the time they reached it Jamie was so keyed up she was ready to scream. The pickup had barely rolled to a stop before she was out of it, and she sprinted toward the clearing near the creek without even waiting for Slate.

She was halfway across before she realized something was wrong. Even then, it took her a moment or two to understand what it was—and when it did finally hit her, she stopped and simply gaped at the trap, unable to believe what she was seeing.

It looked as though it had exploded. The two trapdoors lay askew, and the ground around the pit was gouged away where something had tried to dig up the trap itself.

Jamie swallowed, glanced around the glade uneasily. The sun hadn't reached the valley floor yet and flags of mist wafted through the trees, making her see things that weren't there. Running footsteps pounded up behind her and she spun around, heart nearly stopping.

"Damn it, Jamie. What the—" He saw the expression on her face and stopped. "What's wrong?" Without waiting for an answer, he stepped by her, drew in a startled breath. His soft oath whispered through the frosted air and he pushed her firmly behind him. "Stay there."

"Slate—"

"I said stay put!"

It was the same voice he'd used to control Timber the evening she'd pulled him out of that other trap, and it worked as well on her as it had on the dog. She nodded and looked around her nervously, every instinct prickling with caution.

"It's okay." Slate was looking down into the trap. He eased his weight back, shrugging his shoulders as though releasing the tension in them. He glanced around the glade, rifle ready. "Whatever you caught in this thing didn't stay caught."

Jamie walked over to where he was standing and stared at the destruction in shock. "How could anything have done this?"

"Wood." Slate was on one knee beside the trapdoor. It was still attached to the trap by one hinge, but the other had been torn completely free. "I thought they were all steel."

"It was impossible to get a steel trap in on that road," Jamie said quietly, "so we hauled the timber in and built it right here. But those doors are made out of solid pine, Slate. Ten-by-tens—they're like railway ties!"

"And whatever was in here splintered them like matchsticks." Slate picked up a sliver of wood and turned it in his fingers. "A big bear could do this, Irish. And look how the ground's all torn up—just like a bear throwing a temper tantrum."

"No bear did this." Jamie glanced around uneasily. "Not even Lucifer in his prime could have torn these doors apart like this. And look at the sides of the trap—whatever was in there tore it apart like cardboard."

"Are you telling me you think you caught a Sasquatch?"

"I don't know what I caught!" Jamie stared at the trap, her mind spinning with infinite possibilities. She looked up, eyes scanning the surrounding mountains. They were tall and forbidding and she shivered suddenly, feeling almost afraid of them for the first time in her life. There were places up there that had never been seen by man, hiding mysteries that might never be found. What secrets did they hold, locked in the hidden valleys and crags?

The Indians swore Sasquatch were real, as did her father and thousands of others. Many had actually seen the big creatures. Slate himself—hardly the kind of man to see things that weren't there—had seen *something*. It could have been a big grizzly, of course, but down deep she doubted it. She knew this mountain like her own living room and no strange grizzly could be up here for long without her knowing about it.

She looked up at the mountains again. Flags of snow trailed off the highest wind-ravaged peaks and pockets of ice glinted in the rising sun like goblin treasure. What are you hiding, she asked them silently. What do you know about this that I don't? But they stayed silent, as cold and remote as the moon.

"I don't know what it was," she said more to herself than to Slate. "But it was big."

"Big, and mad as hell—two very good reasons for us to get out of here before it decides to come back for another look." Jamie suddenly spotted something caught in a splinter of wood about a foot below the mouth of the trap. She reached down and pulled the tuft of fur free, fingering it curiously.

"Bear?" Slate squatted beside her, scanning the surrounding trees again.

Jamie ran it through her fingers curiously. "No. Texture's wrong, and the color...it's almost silver." She looked at Slate suddenly. "What color was that supposed bear you saw at the dam?"

Slate's eyes caught hers. "Silver. But it was in the moonlight, Irish. A silvertip grizzly in moonlight—"

"It wasn't a grizzly."

"I thought Sasquatch were black."

"Most that are sighted around here are dark furred, but there have been reports of light-colored ones. Pale brown, silver." She stood up impatiently. "Damn it, Slate. I know you don't believe in anything you can't fit onto a blueprint, but there is *something* out here I can't explain. The last search for Ogopogo—the Loch Ness-type creature supposedly inhabiting Lake Okanagan just west of here—found proof that something very big and very real *is* living in the lake. So why not Sasquatch?"

He stood up. "Jamie, I'm not going to argue with you. Now let's get out of here."

"I want to check the inside of the trap, then I want some pictures of this. And I have to collect the film, and—my God! The camera!" She was on her feet in an instant, pulse racing. The camera was mounted in a nearby tree, lens aimed at the trap, and she licked her lips nervously as she released the bracket and eased it down. "When the trap is triggered, so is the camera. It has one of those silent film drives and it runs off a complete roll, one frame every ten seconds. Some wizard at the university rigged it up to hold a hundred-shot roll."

"That's over fifteen minutes, total." Slate stared at her. "You mean this thing was taking pictures the whole time whatever was in that trap was getting out?"

"With luck." Her hands were shaking so badly Jamie had trouble getting the camera open. She looked at the roll of film. "Of course, whatever was in the trap may have sat inside for an hour before deciding to break out. Or moisture could have gotten into the film and ruined it—that's happened before. Or the camera could have been misaligned and all I've got is a hundred frames of nothing."

"Or..."

"Or," she said softly, looking up at Slate, "I could have the scientific breakthrough of the century."

She didn't find anything else. Although she scoured the ground in all directions, there wasn't a footprint to be found, and that one little tuft of silver fur was the only one her vanished prey had left behind.

Slate was strangely quiet all the way back to the cabin. He seemed lost in thought, a frown lodged between his eyebrows, and Jamie kept glancing at him, wondering what was going on behind those thoughtful amber eyes. He was still quiet when they reached the cabin. He shook his head when Jamie asked him if he'd like the breakfast they'd missed. He dropped into the big easy chair. Leaning well back, he stared into the cold grate.

"Want to talk about it?" Jamie perched on the arm of the chair and brushed a handful of hair off his forehead.

Slate rested his head on the back of the chair and looked up at her. "There's a question that's been running through my mind all morning, Irish. If that film *does* show what you're hoping it does—what then?"

"Well, after the lab in Seattle processes it, Curtis will decide if we've got something worth announcing or not. Then—"

"Curtis?"

Jamie blinked at him. "What's wrong?"

"Nothing." He frowned. "It's just that I thought this was your setup. Yours and your father's."

"Well, it is. Sort of." Jamie frowned fleetingly. "But Curtis is financing it. And it was his idea. If it hadn't been for him, I'd never have done it on my own."

"Why not?"

Jamie shrugged, realizing she wasn't being completely honest when she replied, "Money, primarily."

"Let's say—just for the sake of argument—that you did catch a Sasquatch this morning. And that your camera got the whole thing in living color. Does Curtis mount an expedition to catch the thing? Does he release the photos?"

"Yes. Probably. All of the above."

"And what happens to your Sasquatch then?"

Jamie held that steady golden gaze for a silent moment, then slipped off the chair arm and sat down in the other chair. She'd asked Curtis that very same question not a year ago, and here she was suddenly on the other end of it. "The same thing that happens to any new species of animal," she said, wondering why she felt so defensive. "It will be studied and—"

"How?" His eyes held hers challengingly. "Alive? Dead? Does it get stuck in a cage, or will they just dissect it?"

"Slate, I think you're jumping to some very—"

"I'm just wondering where all of this gets us. Is reducing this thing down to its most basic cells going to stop wars and starvation? Is it going to give us a cure for cancer or—"

"It might." Jamie realized she'd said it too loudly. More quietly, she added, "We have no way of knowing what the impact of a scientific discovery of this importance will be, Slate."

He gave a skeptical grunt, eyes slightly narrowed. "But we know the impact it'll have on Curtis's career, don't we?"

Jamie stiffened. "I don't follow your implications."

"You follow my implications all right, Irish. Don't play dumb with me."

Jamie kept a firm grip on her temper. Damn it anyway. Why was he being so argumentative? And why did she feel so obligated to defend Curtis? "It will mean Curtis won't have to fight for funding anymore. And it probably won't hurt his chance for advancement. It'll open up...avenues."

Slate gave a snort. "A polite way of saying he's not going to have to ride on his daddy's coattails anymore. In fact, it'll probably blow the old man right out of the water."

A jolt of anger ran through Jamie. "Let's just say you're not entirely rational when it comes to Curtis Winthrop and leave it at that, okay?"

"And if they don't catch it, what happens?"

"Then I guess it goes free," Jamie said tartly, "and we rethink the trap design."

"Do you have any idea of what kind of a freak show you're going to have up here if you *do* have something on that film and the pictures get released?" Slate leaned forward and rested his elbows on his knees. "The place will be crawling with every scientist known to man, real and would-be, for starters. Followed by every adventurer, big-game hunter, journalist, TV news crew, monster hunter, huckster, hoaxster and just plain nut case who can get enough pennies together to pay the fare. This whole valley will be so thick with them they'll be walking into each other. They'll be shooting and trapping everything that moves and the local RCMP detachment will spend the rest of its life combing these mountains for the ones that fall off cliffs and into holes and each other's booby traps. They'll chase that thing from one end of this mountain range to the other until they catch it, kill it or just plain harry it to death."

"I think you're exaggerating," she said mildly.

"No, you don't." His eyes held hers. "You know darned well I'm right. What I can't figure out is why you're letting Curtis get away with it."

"Curtis is not 'getting away with' anything." Jamie got up and started tidying a stack of books by her chair. "Didn't you say you had a nine o'clock meeting? It's after ten now."

"They can start without me," he drawled. "Come on, Jamie. Talk to me. Tell me you haven't been boxed into a corner. That you're doing this because you honestly believe that it's right—ethically right. Morally right."

Jamie slammed a book down and looked at him, sparks of anger shooting through her. "I have not been boxed into a corner. I don't even know what you mean."

"You've still got a foot in both camps, don't you? Half of you is still up here in these mountains with your father, and half of you is down there in the city with your mother. You're not doing this because you believe in it. You're doing it because it's what Curtis wants—and part of you figures that by pleasing Curtis, you can please your mother."

"Don't be ridiculous," Jamie said shortly. She turned away and walked up to the kitchen. Damn it, he was doing it to her again! Why did he have to pick away at her life like this, one thread at a time, seeing flaws and knots where there were none? "We're obviously not going to see eye to eye on this, Slate, so leave it alone before we wind up arguing."

"I don't want to argue with you, damn it. I just want you to see what you're doing." Slate followed her into the kitchen and lounged against the fridge, looking down at her.

"I know what I'm doing!"

"Jamie—" He stopped. Stared at the floor as though calming himself. "When I graduated from college, I spent a year working in the engineering offices of a big Texas oil company. One day the owner's daughter came in, and I was seeing stars for a week. We got married six months later. Her father gave us a month in Tahiti for a honeymoon, and the day after we got back he offered me a job in head office. I took it."

He stared at the floor, face hard. "It was a dream I'd always had, getting a solid steady job and settling down in one place. I lasted eight months. By then I couldn't stomach being daddy's protégé any longer. Or the fact that Alison had married me more to shock her friends than out of love."

He looked up, smiling faintly. "I was rough and ready and I'd obviously been around. I had a working man's background—hell, I still had the dirt under my nails. I was something new, something different and exciting, maybe even a little dangerous. She used to drag me to those damned cocktail parties like something on display. Alison's leashed tiger. I knew everyone there figured I wasn't good enough to shine their boots. I just didn't have the right bloodlines."

Slate gave his head a shake, as though scattering memories. "After eight months of shuffling papers, I quit. I got a job with Monolith a week later, and a week after *that* Alison told me she couldn't stay married to a man who worked with his hands and she walked out." He looked up again. "What I'm getting at is that the kind of life I'm living is in my blood, Jamie. If it wasn't, I would have taken to Alison's life-style like a duck to water, glad to be out of the dirt and not interested in ever looking back. And you've got this mountain in your blood just as strongly."

"It's no secret I love this mountain," Jamie said thickly. "I never pretended otherwise."

"It's not just the mountain; it's what it represents, Jamie. Your heart's out here in the wilderness, not down there in the city. It's time you accepted that and quit trying to convince yourself that you can be who you really are *and* the person your mother wants you to be. You can't be two people at once, Jamie. Damn it, I know!"

"I am not trying to be two people."

"Like hell you're not. If you were the woman your mother would like you to be, Jamie, you'd have become an English major and been content teaching sixteenth-century poetry to bored freshmen. But you didn't. You picked up degrees in zoology and biology. You fought for grants to allow you to come up here and study your beloved bears. You live alone in an isolated mountain cabin for months on end with a dog who knows he's really a wolf. You don't think twice about putting on a pack and heading up into the high country for a week or more by yourself. You wear jeans and bush boots and you pack a rifle and you're as comfortable in these mountains as a New York broker on Wall Street. This is *home*, Jamie.''

Jamie turned away, not wanting to hear any more.

But Slate wasn't going to be stopped that easily. ''But you still can't just let yourself accept it and be happy, can you? So you hang on to that teaching job in Seattle, trying to fool yourself into believing that you're up here simply as part of your job. You're always hedging, never committing fully to one life or the other—leave the Mountain and you turn your back on your father; leave the city and you're turning your back on your mother.''

''And just what,'' she demanded furiously, ''am I proving by marrying you? Aside from the fact that I'm obviously crazy!''

Slate looked down at her for a long while, eyes glowing with impatience. ''That's what scares me, Irish. Because unless you make up your mind which side of the track you're traveling, I don't think you'll ever be happy—with me, or with any man.''

Jamie stared at him, suddenly feeling hollow and cold. ''What are you saying?''

''Jamie, until we found that damned trap torn apart, I figured you'd finally let go of the past. But now I'm not so sure. If you're actually willing to sacrifice that animal out there—whatever it is—to Curtis Winthrop's sick need to outdo his father, then you're still not listening to your own heart.'' He gazed down at her, expression quizzical. ''I don't know if you can really love someone until you're whole, Jamie. And you won't be whole until you quit trying to live in two worlds.''

The whole world seemed to be filled with a drumming noise Jamie only half recognized as her own heartbeat. ''Are you telling me that I can either have Sasquatch—or you?''

Slowly Slate shook his head. ''If it were that easy, Jamie, I don't think there'd be a problem.'' He reached across and picked up the roll of film she'd taken from the trap camera. "All the way back here this morning, I was planning to destroy this. I was going to expose it and then rewind it. When you found out there was nothing on it, you'd figure it had been faulty film or a problem with the camera. Then I realized I was kidding myself. Because I don't have the right to make a decision like that for you."

Jamie's face was as pale as alabaster. Slate's heart ached for her, but he couldn't back down now. Pushing her this hard this soon was the biggest risk he'd ever taken in his life, but if he gave in, the only person he was hurting was Jamie herself. If she kept on the way she was, drifting between the two halves of her world, she'd never be certain she'd done the right thing by marrying him.

Always, there'd be the tiny doubts nibbling away at the edges of her mind. A day would never go by when she wouldn't think of her mother's dreams for her, dreams she'd spurned by marrying a nomad dam builder. With those thoughts would come the guilt, the anger. Soon she'd resent the fact that her life revolved around *his* work, that they could never settle in one place long enough for roots to take hold because of *his* dams. She'd spend her days dreaming of what her life could have been if only she hadn't been swept off her feet by the dangerous kind of man she'd always resisted.

She'd become as bitter and angry as her mother had been all those years. Then one day he'd come home and she'd be gone. Like her mother had left. Like his own mother had left. Like Alison had left.

There was no way he was putting either of them through that. Even if it meant losing the only woman he had ever loved, he had to make sure *she* was sure.

"I can't tell you what to do," he finally said quietly. "You have to make up your own mind, Jamie. But I think the time has come for you to make a choice between these mountains and the life you have back in Seattle." He smiled faintly. "Or you can make the choice of making no choice at all, I guess. Whatever it is, it's up to you."

Her eyes were wide and dark and filled with bewildered hurt. "I see," she said in a clipped voice.

"I've got to get in to work." He walked across and gave her a light kiss on the cheek, looking down at her for a moment. Then he turned and did the hardest thing he'd ever done in his life—walked out of Jamie's cabin, maybe even her life, without even a backward glance.

Twelve

She couldn't believe he'd gone.

It had been nearly four hours since he'd walked out that door. Maybe twice that since he'd asked her to marry him. She looked at the rubber washer she was still wearing on her ring finger, smiling at his whimsy. Then her eyes glazed with tears and she closed them. It seemed impossible that in the space of so few hours she could go from such joy to such despair.

The very very worst part was that she didn't even understand why!

She blinked back her tears and looked at the roll of film, turning it in her fingers. And this? What in God's name was she going to do with this?

Right from the beginning, she'd been afraid of this happening. The moment those traps had been set in place she'd been torn between anticipation and horror, wanting to know answers to age-old questions yet hating the very idea of trapping anything wild. She'd lain awake nights struggling with questions, and she'd often wondered what her reaction would be if she actually caught a Sasquatch. Would she be able to sight her rifle on it and calmly plant a tranquilizer dart in the elusive creature, sealing its doom? Or, at the crucial moment, would the scientist in her give in to some romantic urge and set it free?

She'd hoped she'd never have to find out.

"I wish," she told Timber darkly, "that I'd never let Curtis talk me into this in the first place!"

Timber whined, seeming to sense her confusion. He set his chin on her lap and gazed up at her. Jamie scratched him between his ears and he sighed happily. Then his big head suddenly swiveled, ears pricked. He gave a couple of deep-chested barks and bounded into the kitchen to stand in front of the door in anticipation, and Jamie's heart gave a leap.

But it wasn't Slate. A moment later, she gave an inward sigh of disappointment as she watched Sam's muddy green pickup pull into the yard. Timber was gyrating with delight, his toenails clicking like castanets on the kitchen floor, and Jamie pulled the door open and let him out, smiling to herself. As far as Timber was concerned, the only men in her life who deserved to be let in were Sam Two Elks and Slate McCall. He always greeted Curtis with a surly growl and would lie watching him with cold wolf eyes until Curtis finally demanded she put the dog out, and aside from a token tail wag of greeting, he pretty much ignored Terry.

Sam got out of the truck and barely had time to give her a cheery wave before intercepting a flying tackle from Timber. A noisy wrestling match ensued that included a good deal of fierce growling from both of them, and Jamie laughed. She had her mouth open to call to Sam when someone stepped out of the other side of the truck and started walking uncertainly toward the cabin and Jamie simply stared at the figure in open-mouthed surprise.

Her mother gave her a tentative smile, skirting Sam and Timber nervously. Jamie realized she was gaping and hastily closed her mouth. "What on earth are you doing up here?'' Then she laughed and stepped out onto the veranda. "I didn't mean that the way it sounded. It's great to see you. It's just that you're the last person I expected to see."

"I should have called first, I know." Her mother frowned, making her way cautiously across the yard without getting her cream linen pumps any muddier than necessary. "But you know I can never figure out how to put a call through on that radio. Sam somehow knew I was coming in on the float plane and was there to meet me, and he brought me right up."

"Float plane?" Jamie stared at her mother in disbelief. Most people flew in to the nearest landing strip, rented a car and drove the hundred miles to Pine Lake. If her mother had taken the float plane in, things were serious. "What on earth has happened? Is it Granddad? Your mother? You said in your last letter she—"

"No, no. Everyone's fine. I just thought I'd come to visit."

Something was wrong. Her mother had only been up here twice, the last time over eight years earlier. But Jamie simply nodded and held the door open. "How long can you stay?"

Her mother gave a dry smile. "Just for the day. Don't worry, Jameison. I won't interrupt your work."

"That's not what I meant, Mother, and you know it." She kissed the dry, rose-scented cheek. "I'll make some coffee."

She glanced out the window and saw Sam heading for the river, fishing pole over his shoulder, Timber at his side, and felt her heart sink. So this wasn't just a social visit. If Sam was clearing out, something big was in the air. She watched her mother as she wandered around the big living room curiously pausing now and again to look at something that caught her eye.

She spent a long moment looking at the framed photographs on the mantel, then turned and smiled at Jamie. "I'd have thought your father would have thrown all those pictures out long ago."

"He was an incurable romantic at heart."

"Very much like you, in many ways." Her gaze held Jamie's for a moment, then she sighed and gestured awkwardly. "Don't bother making coffee, dear. I came up here to talk."

Jamie swallowed, her heart giving a thump. She nodded and walked into the living room, suddenly aware of her dirty, wrinkled shirt and jeans. Between last night's rain and this morning's work out at the trap, she was a mess. She tried to smooth her flyaway hair as best she could, wondering how her mother always managed to look as though she'd just stepped out of a beauty parlor. Her off-white suit was pristine, even after traveling all day, the perfectly applied makeup was unsmudged, and not one blond hair was out of place.

Her mother sat on the edge of the chair seat, nervous and ill at ease, and Jamie sat on the hearth, wondering why she felt as if she were ten years old again and about to be scolded. "Maybe you'd better just cut to the chase," she said quietly.

Her mother looked up, startled. Then she smiled. "Direct and to the point, just like your father. He always did hate chitchat." Then she sighed and looked down at her hands. "Curtis came to see me a few days ago."

"Curtis?" Jamie's head shot up.

"Yes. He's . . . worried about you."

"Oh, for—" Jamie lunged to her feet. "Worried I might not sell the Mountain to finance his research, you mean."

Her mother looked uncomfortable. "Well, as a matter of fact he . . . did mention something about your not wanting to sell."

"So he sent you up here to talk some sense into me."

"Jamie!" Her mother sounded surprised and hurt. "He did nothing of the sort! As I said, he's worried about you. And he said something about a . . . a man."

Jamie had to bite back an angry retort. "And just what," she said with quiet precision, "has Curtis told you about this *man*?"

"Well, just that Curtis thinks he's . . . well, a little rough around the edges. He works on the dam, is that right?"

"His name is Slate McCall, Mother. He doesn't *work* on the dam, he's project engineer—he runs the whole show. He's thirty-seven years old, divorced, and yes, you could say he's a little rough around the edges."

Her mother blinked, obviously not expecting such a reaction. "And are you and Mr. McCall . . . involved?"

Jamie turned away to hide her smile, tempted for one rash instant to tell her mother exactly how involved she and Slate were. Then the urge to shock was gone and she turned around, looking at her mother calmly. "We're close. Closer than Curtis would like, but that's none of Curtis's business."

"Or mine, either," her mother said with a flash of humor that surprised Jamie. Then she frowned, worry in her eyes. "I just don't want you to get hurt, Jamie."

"I'm not going to get hurt, Mother." Jamie looked away to stare out the window, thinking of Slate. But Slate was gone, and she was already starting to hurt. Once the numbness wore off, she was going to hurt a lot. *I don't really know if you can love anyone until you're whole.*

"I . . . umm." Her mother walked across slowly to stand beside her. "You're not going to do anything foolish, are you?"

"Foolish?" *Only fall in love with a dangerous man. Marry him, if he'll have me. Try to mend a broken heart if he doesn't.*

"Well, it's just that Curtis seems to think this man has some sort of hold over you. That he's trying to pressure you into not selling the Mountain."

Jamie shook her head, smiling. "Mother, Slate doesn't know I've been thinking about selling this property. Even if he did, he's not the kind of man who'd try to pressure me one way or the other." She turned away from the window and leaned against the back of her father's chair. "Curtis is the one trying to pressure me."

Her mother looked at her, puzzled. "I thought you loved Curtis. That you were going to get married."

"I never loved Curtis," Jamie admitted quietly. "I once tried to convince myself I did, but . . ." She shrugged.

"He's a nice man. Solid."

"Safe," Jamie said, completing the familiar litany. She smiled. "Mother, Curtis is a bore."

"Jamie! He's . . . well, he's . . ."

"A bore."

A spark of mischief flashed in her mother's eyes. She smiled, bit her lip to fight it down. "Well, he's . . . quiet." Her eyes met Jamie's and they suddenly both burst out laughing.

"But he's safe," Jamie teased.

"Very safe."

"Why did you marry Daddy?" The question was out before Jamie even knew she was thinking it.

Her mother gave her a startled look. Then she smiled fondly. "I adored him. He was the most exciting man I'd ever met. All he had to do was look at me and I'd melt." The smile faded and her mother shrugged. "That doesn't explain why I married him, of course. I think, if I'm truthful, that I married him to shock the neighbors. I was eighteen and silly, and I was looking for some adventure in my life. The only problem is, when I got it I found I really didn't want it at all. I hated the traveling and the camps, the wilderness—it all terrified me. I missed the safety and security of my parents' home. It was no one's fault but my own, and maybe if I'd been stronger I'd have learned to love it as your father did. But I wasn't strong. So I did the only thing I knew how to do—I ran away."

"Why—" Jamie bit her lip, wanting to ask it yet not wanting to at the same time. They'd never talked about these things before, and she wasn't entirely certain she wanted to now.

"Why didn't we get a divorce?" her mother asked calmly.

Jamie nodded. "You stayed married to a man you couldn't live with for over seventeen years. I never could figure out why."

"You could have asked," her mother said quietly.

It was true. But she'd never dared, was shy even now in the asking.

Her mother sighed. "I loved your father. I guess it never looked that way, but we did love each other very much. We simply couldn't live together." She smiled faintly. "I guess it was my fault. I knew where his heart lay before I married him, but I fell in love anyway and then it was too late. It probably would have been a kindness to us both if we had divorced, but . . . oh, I don't know. We even talked about it once or twice, but it never came to anything. And then there was you to consider. You were bounced back and forth badly enough as it was."

Jamie looked down quickly, old hurts washing through her. *Why?* she wanted to scream. *Why did it have to be like that?*

"Oh, Jamie," her mother sighed. "I know I'm not giving you the answers you want, but I don't know if there are any. Not real answers. Just two people who didn't know how to live with each other—or how to live apart. We spent over twenty years blaming each other for our own failures. Maybe in the end that was what held us together."

"But—" Again, Jamie stopped, not even knowing what it was she wanted to say, to ask. She felt as though she were floating in a sea of confusion, tossed first one way, then the other, trying to make sense out of nothing.

She glanced up to find her mother looking at her with a curious, wistful expression. "I've wondered, these past few years, if I should have just let go. You're so much your father's child, Jamie. I can see him every time I look at you— your eyes, your mouth, even that stubborn tilt to your chin that he had when things weren't going his way. And you've got that quiet, inward strength he had, too." She gave a quiet laugh. "Mind you, I used to think it was just a streak of wayward Irish obstinacy, but as you got older I realized it was the same strength of purpose your father had."

Strength of purpose. That was a laugh!

"I'm so afraid of losing you." Her mother said it so softly that Jamie almost didn't hear it at all. She was looking at Jamie with an expression of desperation. "Every year I could see you becoming more and more like him. Every year you were further and further away, and it seemed that the harder I tried to hold on, the faster you slipped away."

"Slipped away?" It was a cry of anguish, out before she could stop it. "You were the one who kept getting further and further away! Every spring when I'd come up here I was sure I'd never see you again. You'd get all cold and angry the week I was to leave, and by the time I was on the plane I was positive you'd phone Dad and tell him not to send me back, that you didn't want me."

"Didn't want you?" Her mother stared at her. "My God, Jamie, you were my life! What you thought was anger each spring was sheer terror—the terror that *this* would be the year you wouldn't come back. I knew your father would never keep you unless you wanted it, too, but each year you were up here the pull got stronger. I was scared to death that one day you simply wouldn't resist it anymore and would defy both your father and me and stay up here with him. It took every ounce of willpower I possessed to put you on that plane each spring. And if you thought I was cold, it was because I was trying so damned hard not to cry!" Tears glittered in her eyes and she looked away.

Jamie felt numbed and light-headed, trying to equate this woman with the woman she'd thought she'd known.

"I thought that once you started college it would be better," her mother said more calmly. "I hoped you'd meet a nice boy and settle down. When you told me you were majoring in zoology, I wept. I'd hoped once you got away from these mountains you'd get over your fascination with those damned bears, but of course I was wrong." She gave a gulp of laughter that was almost a sob. "Somehow I convinced myself that you'd settle into a teaching job. And when you brought Curtis home that first time I remember thinking that perhaps it was going to work out, after all. I didn't mind it when you came up here to spend time with your father then, because I thought that in the end you'd stick to teaching and get married and live a normal, sane life of the kind most women want."

Jamie had to smile. "Then I got the grant to do this stress study."

Her mother groaned. "I could have killed Curtis! I could see it all happening again. The more time you spent up here, the harder it was for you to leave. I could see it that first fall when you came back. You were tanned and fit and so happy you glowed with it, and as the weeks went by I watched you get pale and impatient and irritable. I knew you were just marking time until the next spring when you could come back up here. I tried to tell Curtis that if he wasn't careful he was going to lose you, but he just kept getting your grants continued."

Jamie smiled again. Poor Curtis. He didn't care if he lost her or not. He simply wanted the traps and all her father's dreams.

"Then he told me about this man you were apparently seeing, and," she said, shrugging, "I had this awful feeling that you had finally broken free and I'd never see you again."

Jamie looked at her, seeing a woman she'd never seen before. "Mother," she said softly, "I love you. How do you possibly think I could just disappear and never see you again?"

Her mother's eyes filled with tears and she tried to laugh, failing badly. "Do you realize that's the first time you've ever said that?"

"That I love you? But you're my mother—!"

"Yes, I am. And I can't remember ever telling you how much I love you, either." Her mother smiled and put her hand out, touching Jamie's hair. "You're so beautiful. Funny. In my mind you're always that little redheaded girl with all the freckles. Then when I see you I can't believe it's really you. A woman, not that little girl anymore."

Jamie didn't even realize what she was doing until she'd stepped forward and felt herself enfolded in her mother's embrace, slipped her own arms around the slim shoulders that were like a stranger's. "I do love you," she whispered, feeling the sting of tears. "I don't always *understand* you, but I love you."

Her mother gave a sob of laughter, fumbling for a tissue. "Heavens, you're the one who defies understanding! How any beautiful young woman can spend her days enraptured by bears is utterly beyond my comprehension. You are just like your father!"

"Do you know that's the first time you've ever said that without making it sound like a disease?"

Her mother stared at her indignantly, then smiled ruefully. "You're probably right. I kept thinking if I fought it long enough it would go away. I should have given in years ago and made both our lives simpler."

"I'm not going to sell the Mountain."

She said it almost defiantly, and her mother waved her hand airily. "Heavens, I don't care one way or the other. Your father left it to you, Jamie. I didn't come up here on a mission from Curtis. I was just worried that . . . well, that I was losing you to some strange man I've never even met." She gave Jamie a long, searching look. "Do you love him?"

Jamie blinked, then let her mouth lift in a slow smile. "Yeah. I love him like crazy."

Her mother nodded thoughtfully. "And is he going to drag you all over the world as your father did me?"

"Probably." Jamie met her mother's gaze evenly. "But I'm going to marry him, Mom," she said firmly, listening to the words as though they belonged to someone else. This couldn't be her, standing here defying her mother so calmly, so easily. "He's everything you warned me against. He's stubborn and annoying and so damned certain he's right about everything that he drives me crazy. And I know I'm disappointing you. I know you want me to get the bears out of my system and wear dresses and high heels and makeup and start behaving like a lady for a change, but I'm going to marry him anyway. I can only hope you'll understand."

"This is not what I came here to hear." Her mother gave her head a despairing shake. "I was hoping Curtis was just overreacting. But . . ." She lifted both hands, let them drop. "Just write once in a while, all right?"

"Mom!" Jamie burst into laughter, giving her mother a fierce hug. "Of course I'll write! And I'm not going anywhere for ages yet. Besides, there *are* things like telephones and airplanes."

"Will I ever see my grandchildren?"

"I promise you'll see your grandchildren," Jamie assured her.

"Just be happy, darling," her mother said with a brave smile. "As long as you're happy, I'll console myself with the knowledge I haven't lost a daughter, I've gained a son who, unlike poor Curtis, can probably change the oil in my car without making a mess of himself. Who knows, one day maybe I'll even forgive him for falling in love with my beautiful child."

"Well, console yourself with this one, too—he dislikes bears even more than you do. He goes charging around like Sir Galahad every time one comes into sight."

Her mother smiled with relief. "Well, maybe this will work out after all. Curtis had me really worried. The way he spoke, you were involved with a dangerous kind of man...."

There were days, Slate told himself as he got out of the truck and walked wearily toward his trailer, that it just didn't pay to get out of bed. Not that staying in bed had much to offer these days, either, since he'd let Jamie slip through his fingers.

God, how he missed her! It had been two long days now, and he was only beginning to realize what he'd done. He shouldn't have pushed her so hard. You'd think a man would know after building dams for the better part of fifteen years that brute force rarely got you what you wanted. You didn't dam a river using strength alone: go straight against the current and your dam will be washed away with the first flood crest. It took skill and planning, knowing how to use the river's forces instead of fighting them, how to deftly balance the tensile stresses of concrete and water and saturated rock. It was like some multilayered, three-dimensional chess game, and he was damned good at it. What he wasn't so good at, obviously, was women.

He pulled the trailer door open and climbed the two steps slowly, so tired his bones ached. His hair was damp and matted from a day under a hard hat and he scrubbed his fingers through it. All he wanted was a hot shower, a cold beer and about twelve hours of dreamless oblivion. Although if tonight was anything like last night, he'd be up pacing the floor until five in the morning. He'd gone out to his truck twice last night, intending to drive up there and try to put things back together again. Yet each time, something—pride, stubbornness, resignation—had held him back. Would he be that strong tonight?

The trailer was surprisingly cool. He tossed his hard hat onto the kitchen counter and pulled the fridge open, grabbed a bottle of beer and was reaching for the opener when he saw the flowers. Bluebells. About two dozen of them, in a tall white vase.

Now what? He swore under his breath, half expecting Dave Brubaker to pop out of a corner, hooting with laughter. The whole damned camp was probably in on the joke by now.

He flipped the cap off the bottle and downed a third of the icy liquid in one swallow, feeling it wash away the dust and weariness. Then, wincing, he pulled off his boots and walked through the niche where the table and chairs were and into the living room.

Jamie looked up from the sofa where she was carefully applying shell-pink polish to each toenail. She smiled, then turned back to her painting, frowning in concentration. "You should lock your door, McCall. A man could get all sorts of unexpected company leaving it open like that."

"No kidding." Slate stared at her, wondering if he'd fallen asleep on his feet. Or maybe he'd run the truck off the road and was in a state of euphoric concussion.

She finished the last nail with a flourish, then capped the bottle and held out her bare foot to admire it. Nodding with approval, she looked up at Slate again. "I hate it when you're right."

"Oh?" He took a cautious step nearer, half expecting her to vanish.

"Yeah." She set her foot on the coffee table and leaned back to look at him. "You were right about me and my mother. You were right about the fact that I'm infinitely happier doing fieldwork than I am teaching. You were right about me and Curtis. And, worst of all, you were right about *this*." She held the roll of film up. "Ordinarily I don't care much for know-it-alls, McCall. But in your case, I'm going to make an exception."

"Oh?" he repeated, starting to feel like a dizzy parrot.

"After you left my place yesterday, I was furious with you. I thought you were trying to force me to make a choice between you and everything I loved—just as my mother had warned me would happen if I got involved with your type. But when I started to think it through, I realized that you— how I feel about you—didn't come into it at all. It was all between me and a lot of stuff I've been carrying around for the better part of seventeen years." She looked at the film thoughtfully. "This is what made me finally understand. Because once I realized what I had to do with *it*, and why, I understood all the rest of it."

"Which is more than I do." He grinned at her, scrubbing his hand through his matted hair again. "What did you do with the film?"

"Nothing," she replied serenely. "Yet." Then, before he could stop her, she pulled the unexposed film out of the roll.

"Jamie!" Slate made a grab for it, much too late. He stared in disbelief at the long streamer of ruined film spiraling from her hand. "But...you never even knew what was on it!"

"I don't want to know." Calmly she tossed the film onto the coffee table. "It may have been nothing at all, or it may have been...well, who knows. I don't want to know because I don't want the responsibility that goes with knowing. I spent all day yesterday trying to decide what to do with it. I kept telling myself that I'm a scientist, that I have a duty to give it to Curtis. Then yesterday afternoon I took a long walk down by the river. I was thinking about my father and how he loved this valley. And I remembered him telling me fairy tales when I was a kid. They were always filled with unicorns and dragons and griffins and elves and stuff, and when I'd ask him if they really existed, he'd say of course— that as long as I *believed* in them, they were real." She smiled, looking up at Slate. "I feel that way about the Sasquatch. Sometimes there's more magic in the dreaming than in the knowing."

Slate gazed down at her, shaking his head slowly in wonder. "I don't know if I have the courage that took," he said softly.

"That didn't take courage," she said quietly. "Coming here and admitting I was wrong took the courage."

Slate sat down and slipped his arms around her, kissing her lightly on the mouth. "I missed you like hell, Irish. Life's just no good without you."

Jamie stroked his cheek. "You look tired."

"I didn't get much sleep last night." He caught her hand in his and kissed her palm, eyes holding hers. "Does this mean you're staying?"

"Do you want me to?" She asked it almost hesitantly.

He kissed her properly then, as a man is supposed to kiss the woman he's going to marry, and as he felt her sigh and relax into his arms, he knew everything was going to be all right. Finally, regretfully, he drew his mouth from her. "I bet I need a shave."

"A little rough around the edges," she whispered, "but I already knew that. And I love you anyway."

"And a shower. I'm hot and I'm dirty, and I stink of sweat and diesel fuel."

"It's incredibly erotic. The people who make men's cologne spend millions trying to come up with that exact blend."

"If I go and have a shower, will you be here when I get back?"

"I could always come with you."

Slate felt his gut tighten. "You could," he said quite agreeably. Smiling, he eased himself to his feet, drawing her up with him. Her eyes were dancing and he felt himself drowning in them, prayed that if he was dreaming he would never awaken.

"I told my mother all about you, by the way."

Slate winced. "*All* about me?"

"Well, maybe not *all*," she said with a chuckle. "But enough. She thinks you're a dangerous kind of man."

"And what do you think?"

"Oh, I think you're a dangerous kind of man, too. But I've decided that's the only kind for me."

"Dangerous men can be tamed." His mouth sought hers, found it with delicious ease.

A long while later, she drew her lips moistly from his and smiled, shaking her head. "There are some things—like dragons and Sasquatch and love—that should never be caught and analyzed. And some beasts that should never be tamed."

"Are you referring to your future husband as a beast?"

"Only in the nicest way."

Slate grinned wickedly and, with no warning at all, scooped her up and tossed her over his shoulder.

Jamie gave a startled yelp and clutched the back of his shirt with a gasp of laughter as he strode toward the bedroom. "Slate! What are you doing!"

"Dragging you off to my lair. Where," he added with a lingering pat on her bottom, "I'm going to do unspeakable things to you all night long." He swung her to the floor, grinning.

"Really?" Laughing and tousled, Jamie slipped her arms around his neck. "Why are we stopping here?"

"A quick shower. Even beasts have a heart—if I don't shave, you're going to hate me in the morning."

"And all those unspeakable things you were promising?"

"Come into the shower with me," Slate whispered, backing her into the bathroom, "and I'll give you a sample...."

"Is there room?"

"Trust me."

She did.

And there was.

* * * * *

Silhouette Desire

1989
IS THE YEAR
OF THE MAN!

What makes a romance? A special man, of course, and Silhouette Desire celebrates that fact with *twelve* of them! From Mr. January to Mr. December, every month has a tribute to the Silhouette Desire hero—our **MAN OF THE MONTH!**

Sexy, macho, charming, irritating . . . irresistible! Nothing can stop these men from sweeping you away. Created by some of your favorite authors, each man is custom-made for pleasure—*reading* pleasure—so don't miss a single one.

Mr. January is Blake Donavan in RELUCTANT FATHER by Diana Palmer
Mr. February is Hank Branson in THE GENTLEMAN INSISTS by Joan Hohl
Mr. March is Carson Tanner in NIGHT OF THE HUNTER by Jennifer Greene
Mr. April is Slater McCall in A DANGEROUS KIND OF MAN by Naomi Horton
Mr. May is Luke Harmon in VENGEANCE IS MINE by Lucy Gordon
Mr. June is Quinn McNamara in IRRESISTIBLE by Annette Broadrick

And that's only the half of it—
so get out there and find your man!

Silhouette Desire's

MAN OF THE MONTH ...

MOM-1

Silhouette Classics

COMING IN APRIL . . .

THORNE'S WAY by Joan Hohl

When *Thorne's Way* first burst upon the romance scene in 1982, readers couldn't help but fall in love with Jonas Thorne, a man of bewildering arrogance and stunning tenderness. This book quickly became one of Silhouette's most sought-after early titles.

Now, Silhouette Classics is pleased to present the reissue of *Thorne's Way*. Even if you read this book years ago, its depth of emotion and passion will stir your heart again and again.

And that's not all!

Silhouette Special Edition

COMING IN JULY . . .

THORNE'S WIFE by Joan Hohl

We're pleased to announce a truly unique event at Silhouette. Jonas Thorne is back, in *Thorne's Wife*, a sequel that will sweep you off your feet! Jonas and Valerie's story continues as life—and love—reach heights never before dreamed of.

Experience both these timeless classics—one from Silhouette Classics and one from Silhouette Special Edition—as master storyteller Joan Hohl weaves two passionate, dramatic tales of everlasting love!

CL-36

FOUR UNIQUE SERIES
FOR EVERY WOMAN YOU ARE . . .

Silhouette Romance

Love, at its most tender, provocative,
emotional . . . in stories that will make you laugh and
cry while bringing you the magic of falling in love.

6 titles per month

Silhouette Special Edition

Sophisticated, substantial and packed with
emotion, these powerful novels of life and love will
capture your imagination and steal your heart.

6 titles per month

Silhouette Desire

Open the door to romance and passion. Humorous,
emotional, compelling—yet always a believable
and sensuous story—Silhouette Desire never
fails to deliver on the promise of love.

6 titles per month

Silhouette Intimate Moments

Enter a world of excitement, of romance
heightened by suspense, adventure and the
passions every woman dreams of. Let us
sweep you away.

4 titles per month

SILG-1R

Silhouette Special Edition®

NAVY BLUES
Debbie Macomber

Between the devil and the deep blue sea . . .

At Christmastime, Lieutenant Commander Steve Kyle finds his heart anchored by the past, so he vows to give his ex-wife wide berth. But Carol Kyle is quaffing milk and knitting tiny pastel blankets with a vengeance. She's determined to have a baby, and only one man will do as father-to-be—the only man she's ever loved . . . her own bullheaded ex-husband!

You met Steve and Carol in NAVY WIFE (Special Edition #494)— you'll cheer for them in NAVY BLUES (Special Edition #518). (And as a bonus for NAVY WIFE fans, newlyweds Rush and Lindy Callaghan reveal a surprise of their own. . . .)

Each book stands alone—together they're Debbie Macomber's most delightful duo to date! Don't miss

NAVY BLUES
Available in April,
only in *Silhouette Special Edition*.
Having the "blues" was never
so much fun!
